Pola

The Mysterious Communications of a Gone Woman

Charles Waite Nauman

Plain View Press
P.O. 42255
Austin, TX 78704

plainviewpress.net
sb@plainviewpress.net
512-441-2452

ISBN: 978-1-935514-65-7
Library of Congress Control Number: 2010938127

Cover design by Susan Bright

Cover art by Caroline Haskin

Acknowledgments

With special appreciation to my wife, artist Grete Bodøgaard, who paves my playground with tolerance and the wisdom of her creative genius.

Out of Marcia Wolf's editing and compelling synchronicity with the content of this subject came important realizations and words that drew confidence and honesty into my experimental reachings.

Thanks to the encouragement of the late Stan Brakhage who, having seen the visual content of the work that led to this novel, embraced it by calling it "a breakthrough in the use of fantasy as reality."

To David Nauman, who, early on, read this with a poetic resonance that let me know I might be communicating.

Preface

"*Where there is a work of art, there is no madness*; and yet madness is contemporary with the work of art, since it inaugurates the time of truth."

From the conclusions of Michel Foucault, *Madness and Civilization*.

"*Histoire de la Folie is the work of a young genius, a work of masterful accomplishment and prodigious and prodigal energy, grasp and daring. No richer, more multidimensional work of cultural and intellectual history has been written — including by Foucault himself. English historian Roy Porter... pronounced that Foucault had been the greatest of historians of psychiatry.*"

From a review by Colin Gordon, Royal Brompton & Harefield NHS Trust, published in *Notre Dame Philosophical Reviews 2007.02.23*.

My underlying passion for writing this novel is to explore, in the most intimate way possible, a narrative relationship between and within what I am calling the '*necessary and sacred unity*' of *Art, Mind and Nature*.

Others have written in a more academic way, particularly Gregory Bateson with his epistemological vision of this *unity*, but I have wanted to dance into it with its constellations of tragedy, art, intellect, mythology and tactile embrace of *Nature*.

In the overriding tradition of the West (particularly since 17th century Cartesian philosophy and 19th century science with the consequent industrial revolution) the rationalizing thought process of the mind becomes split from its genesis with Nature. Some forms of christianism (my word) even advocate mankind's hierarchical superiority to all of Nature, placing dominate Mind on one side and subservient Nature on the other. However this has come about, it appears to many as an irreconcilable split. Interestingly, brain-geographers have mapped 'left and right brain' activity. The 'right brain' being more metaphorically visual and the 'left brain' more graphically rational or logical. The irony is that we have a cultural bias that expects the 'left brain' to explain the 'right brain.' This is probably more complex than asking mathematics to explain art. Though brain waves or brain functions don't explain the split, the phenomenon is a touchstone that elucidates the failure of our communion. In the medical sciences we have given the many ramifications of this bias, this split, a name — "schizophrenia" — and it has become a "socially organized moral category."

R.D. Laing, a psychiatrist, but sometimes called an anti-pychiatrist, observed this categorical split in its extreme manifestations of human 'madness,' and wrote a masterful dissertation of its psychological and cultural dimensions called, "The Divided Self," in which he decried the isolating language of Mind-Body, Psyche-Soma, declaring that the Concept of the Unitary Whole does not exist.

Laing and many others, including Doctors Sigmund Freud and Carl Jung observed inherent healing dimensions in Nature's long dark tunnel of madness. Laing is said to have called madness "breakthrough," instead of breakdown.

Without detailing more, let me say that the above intellectual dallyings are not where the real Pola of this novel began. It began in a more naive way. The coordinates of Laing, Bateson and others became only the map I looked back upon after my wanderings in a more tactile and personal geography.

After the assassinations of Martin Luther King, the Kennedys and others my nightmares were filled with questions of violence. Somehow I was searching for the roots of violence. And then, in my very own backyard, in the rocky forests of the Black Hills, a soldier, a veteran, a fugitive of America's far flung wars was assassinated by an eighteen man posse from that village for doing the most human of things. I went into the village, I went into the woods, I went into the hospitals where this man had been incarcerated. I followed the man who became, in this novel, Valjonni. I wandered with him through the rumors, the hideouts and the artifacts of his six months as a fugitive. I found the bullet slashes in the tree where he was murdered and I finally participated in the posthumous court trial which found that posse grossly negligent.

There was a Pola, Valjonni's secret liaison. Though I know her, the Pola of this novel comes mostly from the 'Polas' I have known in the mental health centers where I have worked doing art therapy with film. It is in that crosscutting experience that I came to realize something of the the socially invoked phenomenon of schizophrenia, that it is a kind of cultural alienation where certain of us seem trapped to act in the most divided of ways. But as R.D. Laing has not only postulated but shown, Nature has a healing vision for its own survival. And for me to tell the unifying vision of Art, Mind and Nature, I would have to find the revelatory, perhaps hallucinatory and healing voices of Nature. Pola has seen Valjonni murdered. Now it is the voice of Pola's madness evolving from the 'split' to a kind of mandala balance that seems to make the healing voice possible.

In this whole process, which we discover through a kind of regenerative communication (Pola with Valjonni), we experience a metaphorical language (not unlike an artist discovering her voice), a language which Pola shares with Valjonni's mud sculptures. It is right-brained illogical stuff, but the shape is purely generative. There is, in this generative meandering a latent and then a more profound search: a search for a recovery of some lost visage, a kind of 'holy grail' of something Valjonni has seen, which may or may not be hallucinatory. But the image becomes both Psyche and Somaesthetic. It suggests a Jungian grasp of the fourth dimension, where the 'dark unconscious' swallows its invader. This is where Valjonni dies. It is also where Pola survives.

The visage, the image, the Mystery Keeper, as it is sometimes called, undergirds the whole story. It is a magical and believable root of the whole Forest. Indeed, such a remarkable somaeasthetic image was found in the forest where the novel's Valjonni died.

Chapter One

Pola, slight and blond. Is dancing. Pola, dazed and euphoric is painting. The grim institutional room where she splats the clay of her feces, where she spins the arc of her commanding gesture is not what Pola sees. This is a pavilion of transforming light – green becomes orange, orange becomes gold. Flames from a center of expanding fractal shapes rise over a dismal, yet invisible cot. There is balance. There is symmetry. The circle is equal to the square. The center is equal to the circumference. Comfort is equal to harm.

Into the opening of Pola's room, which has no door, Cora, a nurse in burnt maroon dungarees stumbles to a sudden stop, gags, moans and turns away more suddenly than she has arrived. Orderlies will return with squeegees and buckets of soap-riled water.

○

In the sun room Dr. Janivik has just finished a round of *group* and lingers with two of the Center's newly arrived clients, one who has chosen the tree on which he will hang himself. The other whose anger will in time explode his heart. Both of them rejected, yet insistent partners in murderous marriages of hate. Calvin, the last one Janivik had listened to, was another classic double-bind: "She," Calvin said, "She said I put her down like shit. I said I didn't put you down like anything. She says, I put her down for *thinking* she was putting me down. That's not true. So what the hell, I said forgive me, for I know not what the fuck you do. Forgive me. Forgive me." Calvin pauses long for emphasis. "She says, No. No. So. I can never forgive her for not forgiving me."

The 'binds' are like so many stones that Janivik refuses to carry away with him, but Calvin's adamant face, his boozled eyes like two pee holes in the La brea Tar Pits become one more *indelible* etched in Janivik's memory of irreconcilable logic.

◯

In the corridor, Emma, the Red Cat Woman (so called by Psych Techs because of her red hair and the way she pounces when she hasn't had her meds) leaps away from a wilting orderly who was expecting to lead her to the drug window. In an ecstatic, traffic cop gyromancy, Cat Woman is fiendish in her boisterous determination to direct some unseen bedlam of traffic to "Heav-en! Heav-en! Heav—"

At the edge, an impatient female Psych Tech hustles Pola to the shower.

Chapter Two

Dr. Janivik is probably too young to tell Uncle Remus stories, but certain divining children, had they known Old Remus, might have seen the kinship. Even as a child his mother had called him 'one of the old ones.' He has the rusty hair of a Scotsman, whose country still claims him. The scatter of freckles on his nearly symmetrical face supports a sense of the regular about him, vaguely disguising the confiding eyes and tilted head of man who hears distant rumbles, or maybe just the finite pleasure of the bassoon. Maybe it's his dialect that so colludes with others, that even a linguist once doubted his Scottish origins as she observed the territorial slide of his voice move from a Woody Guthrie drawl to a Leonard Cohen clip as Janivik tuned his conversational empathies from an Oklahoman to another from Canada. That is until she heard him call a mountain a ben and a scone a bannock. A sculptor he knows in Edinburgh once called him a jaguar with a koala cool.

Though he has already heard about the Pola event, Janivik's composure is unruffled as he enters this disheveled room of four tired lounge chairs, no desk, no computer, a disarray of books on a wall of shelves, which have at the very top a severely cracked Jamon Pottery Horse whose guiltless eyes engage the canted image of a Shiva sketch on the far wall. A lute, a waterphone and a slotted wood drum lay transient on a lower shelf.

○

Janivik meets the brisk arrival of the rattled Cora with a bleak smile. This woman with the broad silver part, the long-thick black-dyed hair, the smell of Vaseline and the spaniel eyes swings one arm like she is coming at him with a rubber dagger.

He takes the clipboard of charts she waves in front of him, but speaks without looking at it. "Wow, this was a good one! She's been off the Ziprasidone — not very long and th ....

" Nurse Cora interrupts. " Long enough to drive the rest of us mad. The whole staff is ..."

But Janivik continues. "This could mean that Pola is already acting out, no not acting out, diving-in to her, her maybe, real journey. Incredible."

Cora cannot fathom this man, this Janivik, his daring to toy with a suicidal woman. "Incredible is not the word doctor. She's painted the wall of her room with feces, she set her mattress on fire... she ..." Janivik looks into her face with pointed curiosity: "What did she paint?"

"With feces — shit! Doctor!"

"No, I mean what sort of design — or what did it look like."

"Look like, Doctor? We forgot to stand back and admire it! A bunch of circles and squares with more circles and squares. The message is, it didn't smell too good."

Janivik is suspicious of his own frail elation when he hears Cora's description: "Circles and squares. Inside of each other?" Has he heard her right. The Nurse's non-answer to his question does not dispute the description. "That could be a mandala! A mandala. Do you know what that could mean?"

Cora has more: "I forgot to tell you, she danced in it ... she painted circles inside squares with her feet." Suddenly looking at Janivik with disdain, she stops in amazement: "No, what does it mean?"

"It might mean she is reaching to help herself." Trying to restrain his hope, Janivik edges toward the corridor.

Chapter Three

In the spacious sun porch of this 1890s institutional structure, with its creaky pine board floors, the twenty-four variously cracked and unwashed windows, the walls are a harmonium of brightness with the flooding blossoms of two pear trees on the green below. They are alone here. Janivik and Pola.

Pola responds easily to Janivik's casual smile. But Janivik has seen Pola as a fragile young women protecting herself under a confusion of identities, primarily the transference in her vision of Dr. Janivik as the young man — 'Johnny.' The one she knew in the forest. Dr. Janivik knows there was such a man, but Pola, Janivik believes, is using Janivik as a sheltering mentor to deny the tragic death of the real Johnny. The Johnny who was killed by a sheriff's posse at Christmas Time.

Wanting to push one step back from that transference today, Janivik hopes to seine something from what might have happened with Pola in the incident of fecal painting and dancing, an incident he finds so loaded with infantile regression and cosmic reaching that he feels a need to censure himself for expecting some epiphany. But when Pola speaks, Dr. Janivik is still Pola's Johnny.

"I'm glad you came back Johnny." Yet, Pola speaking first is not the usual litany. Usually, somewhere in a thwarted cave of rage, in a depression that never drains is where he finds her. Something is different. Her words are like the memory of rain.

Pola: I saw you dancing in that storm last night. Her head nods in positive recognition as her sense of the instant slides and Janivik perceives a woman rapt in some inexplicable presence.

Pola: And out of the storm you found a beautiful piece of light. Yes, the — peace of light —

Janivik: How did you find this ... light?

Pola: You did it for me. Dancing. In the fire-tower. They were hunting you. Hunting you, Johnny and ...

Janivik works to, or is tricked to, imagine some boyish looking Janivik, or Johnny in a fire-look-out, a watch-tower over the forest. But for Pola it is like a movie-screen immediately before her eyes.

Pola: It's that old Cicero tower. You climb it. You are alone. Playing. Throwing your paper airplanes. They sail so peacefully over that rocky forest. On that crackly radio — they are hunting you. Say you have a gun. You have no gun. Funny. You bump your head when you plop down on that tiny little cot. Sleep. But the flash, the bang. The lightning! You wake. You stand. The storm is very loud. Very thunder. Very. Lightning! Balls of fire dance on the rails around you. It is scary. Very scary. You cannot change it. You cannot change it! The walls of glass explode. Echoing. Four-times-four from all the windows. With your hands. Your feet. You chase the echoes. Squaring your house against them. Funny. You cannot change it. You are dancing *with* it. At the center, a table is round and glass. You touch it. Because you are there. It spins. And all that light becomes a jewel. One jewel.

Pola's large eyes quietly scan an invisible space before she continues.

" I guess the storm is over now. Except the sheets of light that hold the sky together with the forest. Quiet sheets of light. Taking you from the windows to. To — where *you are everywhere — the Forest*".

Pola's trance-like presence jogs. She looks through the array of very real windows from this very real and bright sun room. Janivik rises from his chair, hardly able to take himself from the journey. He goes to the nearest window. Looks out at the brilliantly blossoming pear trees, then turns to see Pola. Her face, strong and peaceful. Again, she is the first to speak. "The next morning you looked like that China Guy under the tree."

"The Buddha?" Janivik says.

"I guess. You caught this piece of light and—" Her hand, like a fragile cup, touches the forehead between her eyes, "and left it here."

For Janivik this centered moment of calm suggests an enormous evolution for Pola, and for what he believes bears witness to his sense of anti-psychiatry — a possible drug-free journey out of what he calls the confusion others call schizophrenia. But in that same moment, the moment he wants to say some confirming thing to Pola, Pola's face crumbles from what Janivik saw as near ecstasy, to a shaking blanket of trauma.

"What is it?" he says.

"Run! — Oh!"

A sickening cry, A long soft moan. These are all that Janivik knows of Pola's painful slide back into the Forest: But Pola can hear the sound of her own voice. Screaming. Can see the flash of two rifles. The fleeing man. Falling. Fallen. By the snow edged creek. Members of the posse walking toward him.

Suddenly, Pola stands with the urgency of running, but wakes to the sight of Janivik standing nearly in front of her: An unbelievable phantom — Janivik standing. Standing here. In this bright room.

Janivik can only manage silence. Pola's wide, indigo eyes are at this moment kissed with the clarity of wet marble and convey such a mix of mystery and innocence that Janivik is unable to render.

Finally, the affirmation of his hand slides across the blade of Pola's shoulder and Janivik moves to leave the room. "The 'tower dance' is good news," he tells her. "I hope we can talk again, when you are ready. Get yourself some rest, Okay?" He stands by the door, waiting for her to walk away with him. "The painting on your wall was good news too. I mean, I wanted to see it. But — Cora is going to bring you a bag of colored paints, which you might like. Hey, it's okay to paint on the wall."

Chapter Four

In 1968, for a period of about eight months, Finlay Janivik wandered into a kind of collaboration at Kingsley Hall, East London, with two existentialist psychiatrists. One was R. D. Laing, the author of "The Divided Self," a book that sent Janivik wandering still further into an 'inner-space' dialectic, and into a distrust of the tools and techniques of the conventional psychiatry he had just been trained to profess.

At Kingsley he had encountered a gathering of some extraordinarily free-thinking and sincerely motivated therapists and artists. Basically, they were 'seekers' he thought. Men and women who were knowledgeable, but troubled and suspicious about the authenticity of psychotherapy as it is usually practiced in places of incarceration. Some were people who themselves still wallowed in the inferno so many called schizophrenia. One such person, Mary Sandlin, had moved Janivik profoundly. Hers was a journey that did not happen with drugs or the spasmodic counseling sessions typical of institutions where she had first sought help. At Kingsley she was allowed to regress, bash about, doodle in her shit, and re-grow herself. As Mary later described, she found her way from the false self, to madness, to sanity.

○

Janivik has come to imagine Pola as another Mary Sandlin, someone who might be able to make it all of the way through madness, to sanity. The mandala houses Pola is making for herself, or to tell other people about herself, are surely real benchmarks, Janivik thinks — toward, through, or out of the furious place that lives inside her.

Mary Sandlin had become a furious painter, and had even been encouraged to do her 'spirit-paintings' all over the walls at Kingsley. Storytelling paintings of resurrection and renewal, of darkness and light. Not so different from Pola' s 'Fire Tower' story Janivik tells himself.

○

Finally designated as 'dangerous to herself and others,' Pola had been hurtling through mental treatment centers and from one psych ward to another before arriving at Carduelis. Without Carduelis, the state's Department of Human Services, with less staff and more recidivism than most prisons, was going to be Pola's last stand.

Janivik signed her in at Carduelis, and she immediately tried to electrocute herself by bashing out the breaker-system with a tripod-mounted video camera someone had left in a foyer. Apparently intent on eating the live wires, she was saved by Henry, the gray-shirted building steward, who, rushing to return the place from darkness, splashed blindly into a flare of sparks and into Pola, bringing them both flat to the floor.

In the craft room, Pola later swallowed all of the green clay. Another time she smashed a two gallon pickle jar and was barely stopped from ramming a shard of the glass into her neck.

Routinely, she turned in retreat from anyone she saw coming down a hall or through a door. When she spoke, which was rarely, it was usually to insinuate paranoid epithets on a staff person: 'posse' or 'more posse,' or 'member of the posse!'

○

At Carduelis Janivik is keenly aware that Pola has little chance of receiving the twenty-four-hour care and the merciful support that brought Mary Sandlin through. But Pola is not Mary Sandlin, Pola is re-growing herself, Janivik thinks, from some re-invention of the fugitive life-and-death epic she shared with the estranged, and fated young war casualty, Johnny Valjonni, who couldn't go home again. But most of what Janivik knows about Valjonni is hearsay, or what Pola has thus far shared through what Janivik calls his 'taming down visits' with her.

But now Pola's mandala stories have taken on labyrinthine dimensions. In at least one dimension it is a story which casts Janivik at the center.

Janivik becomes Pola's Johnny Valjonni. This could all be Pola's own creative projection, the classic protective shield of denying the death of her lover, Janivik thinks, but the seeming authenticity of event and detail is baffling. In part of Pola's 'fire-tower-telling' Janivik even felt that it was as though he were actually hearing the story directly from Johnny Valjonni, or from Pola as Valjonni's immediate witness. Yet, Pola could not possibly have been in all those places where Valjonni visited, trespassed or perhaps simply rendered to Pola from his own fantasy life, nor does she claim to have been present. Yet, she convincingly portrays his movement with exquisite detail. Even how he bumped his head on the cot at the tower.

Chapter Five

Janivik parks his nine-year old faded red Toyota in front of a Japanese Restaurant, the Sakura. It's not the kind of place he had expected to find in rural Colorado, but Medicine Springs is not where he expected his attraction to a contemplative environment would lead him. It was on a speaking journey across America he had paused to visit the 'Gateless Gate,' a Zen Center on a plateau north of this little mountain town. And that is where he walked on Rainy Mountain with Romi, her wet face like a private sun. The touch of her hand, a surge of secret joy. Romi, the spirited, the skeptical, the tolerant. Together they now share a 'kipskin' of home-life in a '102 year' old edifice of brick and mahogany —"random renovation" Romi calls it — in the former Springs National Bank, the last bank to close its doors in this ranching, mining and sawmill town of just under 3,000.

○

"Hey, I'm glad I had them hold the sake," Romi says, as she bumps belly and cheekbone with Janivik. She has already ordered for the two of them, a Sakura favorite—Hibachi Shrimp with ginger mustard.

The sake is delivered almost in the instant Janivik is seated. Curiously, Romi snatches the green-glaze carafe before the waitress can pour. Pinching her eyes at the glaze — "Its really celadon pottery," she exclaims. Stretching her arm to the two delicate cups, she pours the sake while stealing an introspective blink toward Janivik's buffer of composure. "What wonder of psychiatry is your mistress tonight?"

"It's never psychiatry or mistress. It's something else. Today Pola danced another Mandala, or told me how somebody she thinks is me danced one on a fire-tower."

"Sounds complicated. Didn't know they could be danced."

"The best ones may be dances, but they usually go unseen. They may last a minute and nobody witnesses. In London we had artists who encouraged dance, and sometimes we would see spontaneous lotus flower expressions, reflections of yin-yang and such. Some that looked like centered circles of light or fire. We had one fellow, who wouldn't dance, but watched the others with great interest, and finally said he liked the ones that were doing quantum physics."

"Funny," Romi says.

"A little over my head, what he was seeing, but when some of us talked about it, it seemed remarkably credible: 'proportion, frequency and magnitude in one balancing act.'"

"Have you seen them here, Romi asks.

"What Pola does is the closest thing. They are all sedated you know. "Switched on to their 'keepers', and nothing happens!"

"Then why did Pola perform?"

"Against the judgment of nearly the whole staff, I took her off all drugs. And, of course she's been terribly messy and dangerous. A great trial to the nurses and staff I'm afraid. So I'm not very popular down there at the moment. They still sneak the tranquilizers to her when they can, but I think she is on my side now. That's because she has made this enormous transference, this misappropriation of personalities. It happens, too often, to people deep in the trauma of panic. Anyway, I'm her buddy. Out there in the forest where most of her stories wander, she sees me as the guy she lived with. The guy she saw shot down in front of her eyes. But the amazing flip-side of that is, He, this Johnny Valjonni, or her portrayal of him, is doing the therapy. I'm like a witness, but also the 'real guy' in her stories."

Janivik's assumptions seem cavalier to Romi. And her voice sounds uncomfortably defensive when she speaks, "Still they are all *her* constructions."

Janivik nods, but not with the assurance Romi had expected. "Of course, but the detail is so first-hand and amazing. I'm really being sucked into this Romi. I wish I knew more about the guy, this Johnny Valjonni. All I have is that fucking psych history report from Ft. Belvedere where he was incarcerated with, maybe, PTSD after his release from the military and subjected to the usual naming ceremonies, Paranoid, Schizo, I think they even said Autistic. Then doped him and sent him away. The post traumatic stuff was a lot different than I've seen. In counseling they wrote: he screamed and ranted irrationally about: they gave him a presidential citation for killing babies. Other thing I read says his patrol was caught in sniper fire at edge of a village when air-support, he said... 'snuffed it (the village, I guess) with yellow smoke — and all I see is burning shadows,' he tells a counselor ...'burnin' shadows, runnin' with babies swingin' from their arms.' That's the guy Pola obsesses about," Janivik concludes.

Outwardly, Romi and Janivik might be studying the carafe on their table, but it's the image of burning shadows that stokes their silence.

"I'm new to this military language," Janivik says, "but a vet at Carduelis tells me a Presidential Citation is a kind of medal your whole squadron or unit gets for being in the wrong place at the right time. I don't know. This soldier was in pain for something he didn't personally do, but the 'citation' honors him for doing it."

"That image, the scar no one sees, is horrible enough but ..." Romi weighs her thought, "but isn't it curious, putting it into that anguished context, I mean, for me, that anguish, that schism of responsibility is exactly the irony of war."

"I'm sure not many grunts would look at it that way. They might be honored," Janivik says, "or ignore it like all the other bureaucracies of the military and war."

Romi shakes her head. "But this is like listening to the tip of an iceberg here. This man was on the edge and he wasn't talking irony like me. He was talking pain. It's his pain that was realizing the connection."

" Janivik looks at Romi like she was a photograph he had not yet seen, "Yeah, some people can use their pain to connect. I wish they all did. But Pola's connection, with this guy in the forest, her behavior— it's like a synchronicity she might have had with him and still hangs onto posthumously. And its changing her."

Romi's dark Asian eyes focus in their usually, quiet and steady way when she knows Janivik's quest might also be hers. "John Valjonni. I want to know about him, too. Wouldn't there have been an inquest?" She thinks that Janivik is pleased with her curiosity, then sees him glancing at his watch —

"I need to spend more time with her. She is there. Like. In a cradle. 'Time and the human heart.' " It's a paraphrase that makes Janivik feel very lonely, perhaps because it is both too simple and too hard. "I asked for it, and now that's really the best we can do for her."

Romi repeats, "Time and the human heart." She had hoped that some of that 'human heart' would be with her tonight. "Tonight?"

He nods.

"Can I," she hesitates, "see her?"

This is not really the professional thing at Carduelis Janivik reminds himself. Yet at Kingsley the personal thing would have been the right thing. He smiles. "Might help her identify me."

Chapter Six

At Carduelis, Romi, Janivik and Pola have been sharing in a loosely bantering conversation, while taking turns at sailing poker chips across the rug of Janivik's Room of the Broken Horse. The chips bounce around the rim or into the cozy funnel of a Pima Indian basket near the far wall. Romi laughs, "I said if I make three in a row, I get to take you all to lunch one day." Her chip hits the rim of the basket and caroms in with Romi's flashing smile. "I did it, I did it," she cheers. But, for the whole evening Pola's eyes have hunted Romi, and Pola's expression doesn't change much even now. Yet she has heard the unexpected, that she could go out into the real world, away from the confines of Carduelis. She looks wonderingly at Janivik. "You mean we can go out?"

"Of course. It would be fun, don't you think?"

Pola, not entirely free of suspicion, looks at them a second time, "I didn't. I — yes!"

Romi moves to the door. "Well, I go now." She turns to Pola with a hopeful smile, their eyes briefly catching. Pola studies Janivik as Janivik watches Romi's departure down the hallway. When he turns back to Pola, he sees a face troubled with some big question. "Is that Ramona?" Pola says.

"Romi," Janivik corrects.

"Because I want to know who she is!"

"Romi?"

"Ramona! Is that Ramona!" The tantrum response confuses Janivik. They look at each other. Her silence is fraught with some kind of searching urgency. Janivik considers probing.

"Tell me who you mean by Ramona.

Pola glares. "No."

"Be Ramona. Be Ramona. You — be — Ramona."

Pola's whole face appears to blink and linger on that question. She has done these role-playing therapy games before, but this comes to her not as Pola role-playing, but, like the tower mandala, as Pola projecting her vision through Valjonni's vision:

"Ramona ... when she is in the Town, she is like the Town ... when she is in the Forest, she is like the Forest." Pola's voice wanders off mysteriously. Her eyes focus again to that screen of her transcendent vision; and to the ghostly-dual-mediator of that vision, Johnny Valjonni: "He is walking in the forest, deep into the big stone quarry. The walls are crumbling, falling down. His mother — Pola's eyes go shut. No, the Stone Mother is there. Behind the falling rocks. And. And, below, made of clay: the man and woman, making babies. They are fucking, fucking, fucking .... Into the tunnel with dark and burning trees. Below the sky— every tree is burned and black. The whole forest. Ramona, that Indian girl. She is dressed in something short. She brings him water. She takes the glass when it is empty and disappears behind a stone. Johnny wants to find her, but when he goes behind the stone, she is gone. But, there — with every black-burned tree — are her sisters. His sisters? Ramona's? I don't know. Oh! He wants to find Ramona. He is happy. Oh, he is not happy. He is in the Town. She is in Cambria. She laughs at him. In Cambria she laughs at him, hates him. Calls him 'blue-eyed' Indian. The sawmills are cutting him. The noise is loud. Is awful! Cutting him."

Pola brings her hands to her ears. She is crying. Pola opens her eyes. Sees the Broken Horse. Sees she is still in the Room of the Broken Horse. She stares at Janivik. "They took your job, Johnny."

"I'm not Johnny. I'm Janivik, Pola." Pola whimpers. Looks at him sideways. Whimpers.

Chapter Seven

This transference thing, making Janivik into Pola's lost lover, it's gotten into her head, Romi knows. Is it possibly dangerous? Something amorous developing with Pola and Janivik? Profound relationships? They've been known to percolate right into a complicated dedication like theirs. Doctor and patient. She's heard such stories, even from Janivik. But no. Romi is unwilling to embrace those stories. The best thing, the strong thing is to embrace the enigma, whatever really happened to Pola, whatever really happened to Johnny Valjonni.

The slack moment of uncertainty, that weird little preservation instinct cannot be part of this, she tells herself.

Chapter Eight

When Romi comes down the steps of the quarried, rust and soot stained stone of Springs County Court House, she finds it too easy to imagine that this building was here as recently as 1913, marking its authority over the helpless coal miners, their wives and children who were massacred in a tent camp a few miles away at Ludlow. These steps would have known the shadows of those thugs, the hired cops, the governor's police, the National Guard, the sheriff's posse so willing to fire randomly and purposely into the shelters of the defenseless.

These are people, she fears, who have not changed much in the years since Ludlow. What she has seen in her gathering of court transcripts and inquest documents surrounding Johnny Valjonni's death confirms this. Yet, even in the transcripts, there are some interesting exceptions to this vigilante flag, she notes. There was in the posse of that final hunt, which surrounded and killed Johnny, a State police officer who fired his rifle into the sky to warn Johnny, and reported Johnny's last words: "Stop or I'll kill myself." There was Norton, the stone mason, who went to the mortuary after Valjonni's death. Put his hand in the wound that killed Valjonni. Reported the bullet had entered from his back. And there was Kate, Pola's aunt and proprietress of Kate's Gold Pan Saloon, where the hard-rock miners and sawyers of the stump-grazed forest and the sawmills, that once included Johnny, still come regularly.

Chapter Nine

Kate, red hair, a dark mole below the crest of her broad cheekbone, a smile too gentle for the raucous, beer swilling demons who come out of the forests and the mines each night. A silver studded denim vest hangs loosely over her checkered green and tan cowgirl shirt. It's a busy night, but her smoky-green eyes trace quickly to acknowledge Romi sliding onto a stool near the center of the long laminate bar. She doesn't know Romi has driven to Cambria to meet her. But like a good auntie, Kate will be there, a reservoir waiting to be tapped by any outsider whose opinions won't spoil her own precious details.

The reek of alcohol from the sawdust drenched floor suggests to Romi that red wine is not the usual drink here, but when she orders Kate tosses a stale looking bottle with a loose cork under the counter and brings up a cheap generic burgundy with only a screw cap. It's late, even for the Gold Pan, and Romi scans for the atmospherics as they might have been for a solitary figure, a Johnny Valjonni, seated here where she is at the bar. He would have been drinking a beer she thinks. She catches Kate. "I'm switching to beer."

"You don't want the wine?"

"I want what Johnny Valjonni would have been drinking here tonight." Kate is slowed to a double-take, half of it conjuring the ghost of Valjonni and half keening some unexpected ghost of empathy.

Romi, wishing not to be the full-suited voyeur, is still a voyeur — listening to the jargon, looking at the ethnic mingle of untamed faces. No faces like her own — the direct descendant of parents who had survived the Japanese prison camp just across the border in Wyoming. Most likely they haven't even heard about the internment camp. She knows this from other times when this was mentioned. Her linguist training listens hard for the old world and new world artifacts of language, but here in loose tongued monopodes they have not just peppered the language, they have paved it with scatology. Even the metaphors, which feel like they are almost being invented before her eyes, are pure scatology, she discovers. Like the sallow-faced guy whose one ear wiggles a convulsive rabbit-twitch when he listens to a crack about a tourist who didn't know 'green turtle shit,' and responds about the ranger who is so level-headed 'the shit pours evenly out both ears.' 'Yeah, but he wouldn't know a enough to dump it outa his own boot,' she hears the first one conclude. Romi has one more beer and looks in the mirror to the end of the barroom. The Indian girl.

○

The last shattering tumble of hollow bottles into the drum of a plastic bin and the country tunes of Elly Fay — "They Took My Man Away," fade into the boozy din of stale smoke and the humming silence of neon and cooler buzz.

They are alone, and Kate's rambling vignette of images attack Romi like flashback-cinema, pivoting on the characters Romi has only moments before witnessed — that barroom stage on the other side of her beer bottle.

Kate: "His eyes followed that Romona, that cute little Indian girl. Wherever she sat, he would watch her in the mirror, or even follow with a case of beer up that outside stairway to her room back here in the alley. But, I don't think she ever let him in. She called him a 'blue-eyed-Indian,' and that's what he was. It seemed like he was always on the outside of something – on the edge. Half here, half there. They tell about the night he got fired, laid-off at the Cambria Sawmill. How he got accused of chaining the sheriff's car to the bridge, when all he was doin' was cutn' down the alley and saw those goofs who were doin' it. I would a watched, too. And then, couple days later, old sheriff Blaine, always watchin' him, sees Johnny releaving himself in an alley just barely in site of the Dew Drop Inn, where the sheriff and some school kids was buy'n that soft ice cream. He actually arrests Johnny. Thinks its his duty, I guess, to protect all human beans from the sight of it." Kate pauses and looks a sudden question at Romi: "How come. I don't know, but you sat in the same place Johnny always sat. Then, you ask for his beer. How come. Did you know him?"

"No. I met Pola. At Carduelis. She talks about him. Like — he's inside her head."

"Oh. Pola. My niece. She's my niece." Kate pauses, looks steadily at Romi. Her green eyes seem suddenly gray, grief-worn, grim. "There was never such a broken heart. She saw him murdered. Justified homicide is what the town calls it. Lot of us know better. He was shot in the back at close range by crack marksmen from the State Troopers. Eighteen posse, mostly off streets of Cambria. They gassed him outa that cave. Chased him like fox hounds. 'Til at the last he pulled that empty ancient, useless pistol outa his jacket and pointed it at his own head. Said, 'Stop or I'll kill myself.' That's what Pola sees in her head all the time. That's what drives her mad. She would say the same thing — even act it out. All of a sudden, act it out. On the street, post office, most anywhere: She puts her hands up like this," Kate puts her two hands together, prayerfully, fingertips touching just beyond her chin. "That little gun with the broken trigger was, like between these hands, but pointed at his head. 'Stop or I'll kill myself.' They — one of the cops, the one who shot in the air — heard it, said it in court: 'Stop or I'll kill myself,' that's when they shot him." Kate pulls herself up, wants to cry, wants to burst with anger, but the empathy, perhaps the neutrality she senses with Romi loosens the burden, opens this path to Pola. Pola.

Kate's eyes brighten, focusing and re-focusing. Romi could imagine a mother ready to say something wondrous about a gifted child.

"But Pola," Kate says, "Pola was his secret. And he was hers. Pola brought him food. He brought her The Forest. 'Not like words,' she would say, 'the Whole Forest.'"

"She told you a lot, I guess."

"No. Not really. She didn't tell me nothin' at the time. Not at all. Not at the time. Like I say, it was a secret she kept even from me. For six months the sheriff and his posse was huntin' him. It had to be secret. She would take him birthday cakes, everthin'. I never knew. She wouldn't tell. She was hidin' him. They never figured to track her. They was always look'n to track Rita, his mother. She was gettin' his veteran's disability checks signed. Bert, that blond, baby faced sawyer you might a seen at the table behind you tonight – I know he brought Rita out there a couple a times. She wanted to bring Johnny home with her. And, she wanted him to take the drugs the V.A. was send'n him. Do you know, the state can actually force you to take drugs. Rita wanted to do this. But Johnny was afraid he'd end up in the saws if he took 'em when he was still workin' at the Cambria mill. Pola saw him throw the pill bottle Rita brought him half-way 'cross the forest one time, then turn around and crash and thrash every stick and stone in sight.

"The thing is, Pola understood the special part of him. Understood — somethin' — I'm gonna say, somethin' sacred."

Romi wants to ask Kate what she means, 'sacred,' but sees closure. Some territory of forbidden travel stumps Kate, Romi thinks. Or does this conundrum of madness only speak in Pola's Voice?

34

Chapter Ten

A waterfall spreads down a ragged cliff of layered rock forming a thinly glistening, torrential veil as it rushes into a broad pool at the bottom of a cliff. From a hidden niche behind the veil Romi bursts into the pool, nude and dazzling in the late rays of sunlight; peals and scans back expectantly into the roaring falls as Janivik bursts like a second porpoise into the pool with her. Together they roll with unabashed nakedness, laughing in the thrill of wild-water. In the gambol of a floating embrace they nearly sink below the surface, but rise together, laughing. Janivik pauses, treading, curiously intent on a very tiny whirling-eddy of white substance. Janivik laughs and calls to Romi, "What is this? You leave this here?

Romi floats calmly to the thing that Janivik sees. She is quietly astonished: "Sperm. Your sperm."

"Our sperm," Janivik says, "What do we do with it now?"

Romi smiles, some delicate amusement is clearly in her eye. "Is this a philosophical question?"

Janivik squints impishly with his nose. "Not philosophical — universal maybe?" He gestures carelessly over the pool. "That whole mess out there, seedpods, broken roots, helterskelter —" He slaps the persistent spermatozoa with his flat hand, spreading it to the riffles of the pool. "It's all the same, don't you think?"

Romi: "All the same — equal?"

Janivik: "Why not?"

Romi: "What if we're mutating with the fish?" They look about.

Janivik: "I hope so."

They laugh and porpoise to the other side and back.

In their nudity, Janivik and Romi crab their way up an incline of slippery and jutting red rock to a place near the top of the falls where a glass-thin sheet of warm water slides beneath their resting bodies, her sweet porta, his ragged sac. Their quiet is directed to the pool, below — the silence of what they feel, the sound of what they see.

"Kensho," an unthought word spurts from Romi.

Janivik smiles quickly, "You in Japan again?"

"No. Just that Zen thing. Means some kind true nature— wakening. You know — talking about sperm ever where — 'Kensho.'"

Janivik smiles. "Okay." From her glance he sees Romi sifting her thoughts.

"You've had long days with that Pola girl."

"Long months. Like running a nursery."

"I tell you, her auntie thinks — something sacred about her."

"What everybody thinks is important. What everybody does, or has done with her helps unweave the knot. But she still gets into this transference confusion. When she saw you, you became somebody, an Indian girl she calls Ramona. A whole story. A kind of paranoid fantasy that wells up in the present, then goes back to the cave for healing. I can't explain. Call it regenerative communion or ..."

"But there *is* a Ramona. I saw her at Kate's. Kate told me about her, about Valjonni — about Valjonni following her in the mirror of the bar, out into the alleys — like she was hot in his head. But she, Ramona, is Valjonni's story. What can Pola tell you about Valjonni's story? Was he teasing Pola with some kind of bullshit stuff?"

"Not that kind of stuff. Like intimate, worshipful stuff. Like a movie, all the little details— seeing it through his eyes. It's like *his* fucking story! If it were his story I could see it as the disenfranchised Indian boy he must have been — reaching for the lost generation of his people or something. But, it's the Forest, it's the Rock, it's — god, if I could tell you what she is saying, or seeing, or reliving, or ....

Janivik leaves off, quietly looking at the darkening sky, seeming to thrust wonder into the silence before he speaks again. "We have to go." But they don't go.

Janivik starts up again. "If I were listening to Valjonni — the way she translates, I would have to call it a great survival trip. His or hers, or his becoming hers. I don't know. But what you have told me about his life in Cambria, where they couldn't see what the war had done to him, tormented him for every little paranoid, eccentric aberration: Accusations that were not about him, like the night when he stands watching two pranksters chain a police car to a light pole. Or smashes his bike to pieces in front of a cop, because the cop is threatening to take it away from him — for reckless riding!? Finally he pees on the street in broad daylight — a perfectly normal thing to do in a town that runs him into the ground at every direction.

"So, their Justice of Peace was going to send him to the shrinks at Ft. Belvedere. Or, if he fights that... put him in jail for thirty days. Valjonni wisely chooses jail. And successfully escapes. Heads to the forest. We know very little about his war scars, except that no one could see them. We are only getting to know Cambria's and — Pola's story. It's her story of him that dreams its way into the forest and into my head in a way I could never have imagined."

It is a dark sky, and the moon has almost disappeared behind the blackening, ink-edged clouds now speeding away from the distant flicker of sheet lighting. Their images of each other dance like whittling pieces of light and nakedness as they search over the rocks for their scattered garments. But Romi pauses sharply:

"You see your — this, Valjonni as a survivor? You said? He died. They killed him! You're telling me what Pola said he did. Her fantastical stories. Janivik, this is not Valjonni!"

"From what you've learned in Cambria, and what we've have learned from Pola, the stories about Valjonni tell me a lot about an injured person who got well. Of course, a lot of good it did him."

"How do you know he got well?"

"I don't really. It's just that he made such a great survival trip, and it was a lot more than just physical survival. The stories that Pola tells of him are almost always regenerative and balancing. And how Pola connects with him is how I see her survival."

"His death was tragic."

"Maybe."

Such ambiguity troubles Romi. She stares critically at Janivik's arching comment. It's a comment Janivik feels hopelessly unable to explain, and yet he heard himself say it.

Chapter Eleven

Awake in bed most of that night, Janivik tried to revive a piece of his own dream, a piece he was sure had repeated itself during his long and enigmatic contemplation of Pola's imagery. It always ended with something archaic, something primordial that was always just beyond his grasp, his vision to comprehend. It troubled him that it seemed so linked to, or maybe just triggered by, Pola's most repeated vision. An hallucinatory something that also went to some incomprehensible place. Janivik tried to play her dialog over again in his head, but he wasn't sure whether it was Pola's story or his own dream. In her story, of course, she always wore the *Valjonni mask*. It started with the mushrooms Valjonni ate from a squirrel's nest. From there she sees him limp and sick on the banks of a mountain stream, drinking heavily of the fresh water. There, on the threshold of dying and living, Valjonni sees a dark snake on the other side. A dark snake, also drinking. Also seeing Valjonni drinking. A *'diamond-being,'* she said, a *liquid* diamond-being flickered and ricocheted between Valjonni and the Snake, and Valjonni the Man entered into the King of the Underworld, entered into the vision of the snake holding vaguely the man. Then within the ricocheting trance Valjonni sees a sphinx-like root, a root stranger than any gnarl he had ever seen. It had four, maybe three faces, but it was changing. Helplessly he felt drawn into its eye, into a vision of a master he must know, but a master who was always on the other side of darkness, hiding in a mystery equal to the closed book of death in life. Awake, but still with his eyes closed, Janivik tries to make meaning of this repeating phantom. "Oh my God," he whispers to himself: *is this Valjonni, Pola or me? She didn't say 'King of the Underworld' It's in my DNA. That D.H. Lawrence 'Snake' poem. It's in my DNA.*

Yet, Pola, or *Johnny,* did speak of a snake and a mysterious-something that he called the *four-in-three*. Its content is fourth-dimensional, Janivik thinks. That extremous place where martyrs go when they become true martyrs. The place of crucifixion and assassination. That place beyond the acceptable polarity of rational psychology.

Janivik's imagination races through the historic symbolism of fourth-dimensional-psychology. Why is that dimension, which he wants to call the 'deep unconscious' always so obscure, so just over the horizon. Somehow alchemy and fairy tale and mythology have always asked the same question. Plato asked that question of Socrates: "One, two, three — but, my dear Timaeus, of those who yesterday were the banqueters and today are the banquet-givers, where is the *fourth?*" Carl Jung's answer to that question was that the fourth remained in the realm of the dark mother, caught in the wolfish greed of the unconscious, which is unwilling to let anything escape its magic circle save at the cost of a corresponding sacrifice. Jung also said that "Timaeus" links chronologically with Ezekiel's vision of the four figures, which reappear in the four evangelists. Three have animal heads and one has a human head — the angel. "Ezekiel saw the wheel way up in the middle of the air, the big wheel run by faith and the little wheel run by the grace of God ..." and all of that. So is this what we in our psychological meanderings call the animus and the anima, those shadow images of the male and female unconscious, which together would be *wholeness?* Janivik is wary. Is this Pola, or myself, or both of us bent on some alchemical resolution? Is this something visible, tangible? Something Pola could hug? Something Valjonni needed to find? Jung's mythology of "sacrifice" and Valjonni's death eerily propose that he found what he was looking for.

Chapter Twelve

Pondering the inchoate image of his dream as he came to Carduelis that morning, Janivik thought of it as a kind of rune-stone of revelation that both he and Pola were still searching. Indeed, Janivik was hardly out of that mesmerizing night when he realized Pola was in the room with him.

In the Room of the Broken Horse Pola's face emerges. She is not in institutional clothes — a high-neck beige sweater with three buttons open to a pale blue shirt, her unwashed light blond hair is vaguely streaked into a flat taffy brindle falling halfway to her shoulders in a hit-miss razor-trim. Her head is cocked as though to hear what the mind of her eye tells. Janivik listening, again seeing it almost like cinema, which he has come to know is Pola's way of telling:

"...she's the one in the gold-lame and the cowboy hat — at the big party. Your Mother Woman, Rita, trick-rope woman, boasting her fame at the 'Garden'. And you, Johnny – cool white shirt, blue jeans. You're in jail. How can you be there? But you *are* there. Already slipping away from that town, from her. That Gold Lame Mother, follows you to the edge ... to the land of no-trespass.

"She cannot enter. But you enter. They are dark. They are quiet. They are your Lakota people. That's your father, Johnny, up there. Beside him, the empty chair. Oh! And Ramona! Ramona with the wine glass. Her middle finger going up and down, exploring the stem. Smiling at you. Then you smile at her, and you are holding hands. Disappearing down the long, dark stairs. You are gone. Up there at the top, frozen in her gold-lame, Rita cannot reach you.

"You are gone. Gone with the naked Ramona: You pitch that leather ball to her. She swings your bat. She is running. You follow. You are going to touch her. But. But she is a buffalo. She takes you to the Forest, where you had to go. And leaves you. Leaves you. Where you had to go."

Pola clearly takes comfort from this exchange: 'Ramona for the Forest.' Her demeanor lightens. She is no longer in that separate reality. Her focus turns pointedly to Janivik, even half speaking his name:

"Janivik — Johnny? And that is when you made the break from jail. You told me that. Just so plain, like the day it happened."

Janivik interrupts: "Can you call him Johnny Valjonni? I am not the Johnny who broke from jail. I am Janivik, your helper, and even I have heard that Johnny Valjonni escaped from that jail. Maybe you can tell me what *that* Johnny told you. Like, how did he — Valjonni — get to the forest. I guess he would have told you about that one of those times you met him out there?"

Pola ponders.

Janivik realizes Pola can still not acknowledge that she has made Janivik her Johnny, yet he watches something bitter flash from her eyes — sees her struggle to let go: "Johnny Valjonni. Johnny Valjonni," she repeats. It's still tentative Janivik presumes, but what comes next is like everyday talk, a story twice-told:

"Johnny knew that for the garbage-guy they would open the cell door. And that's when he did it. Said he shot outa there like a bullet, knocking everbody down. Then, the luck of the Irish, a logging truck, a load of long trees sticking out. He grabbed the longest tree, and swung himself right into that moving load of logs. Said he even watched a sheriff's car go by. Then at the Cambria mill, where he knew the logs was going, he jumped and hid 'til dark between those ricks of lumber. That night, in the light of that big sawdust burner he crabbed his way out of there. Found the steel rail of the old track, and followed it. All the way into the forest. In morning — he saw two helicopters ratting over him, but he could just lay in the shadow of those big granite rocks." Pola breaks off. Shrugs her shoulders. Janivik thinks he sees a kind of disdainful, 'so what' expression move across her face.

Janivik glances toward the crack in the doorway noticing some staff and clients moving together down the hall. "They're going to the dining room. How about you?"

Janivik rises, moving toward the door, hoping to have some more time with her.

"I'll go with you." She doesn't rise.

"No." Her anger levels at Janivik. "Why did you take him away from me?" Cora, the psych-nurse, opens the door gently and promotes a smiling invitation. Pola's question stumbles on Janivik at the wrong moment. Not a good time to end their dialogue. But snubbing Janivik is written on Pola's face as Cora ushers her away, and Janivik lets the moment slip. Say something, say what? he asks himself as Pola passes through the door: *Something*:

"Pola. Don't say we took him away. Say— say, Pola is coming home."

Outside the door Janivik hears the burst of her anger: "That's not home, you idiot!"

○

In the rattle, and steam-soured smell of the dining room Pola stands aloof by a window, watching Janivik get into a car with Romi. The little red Toyota moves to the street. Pola, still watching. Fists of anger and depression clenching toward the corners of her mouth.

Inside the Toyota, not much is being said. Romi wishes she could shake him out of it. That place she knows is still with Pola. Then Janivik speaks. "She just called me an idiot. I trapped her into speaking facts, instead of fantasies: Seeing for a moment that Valjonni is Valjonni, not me. She doesn't want his history, she wants his mythology, her mythology of him, or — whatever this grand story of hers is."

Romi shifts the car onto the highway and into a dazzling sunset. Adjusting her view under the visor, she looks like she could be speaking to the sun. "Thought that was the healing stuff."

"To a point. But when is she coming back?"

Adjusting the visor again, Romi flashes a smile. "I was going to say something about a glass of pinot."

He looks at her with resignation and silence.

Chapter Thirteen

At Carduelis Pola pushes her face against the darkening glint of the double window in the dining room, her fists pressing a burning sky of meteors into the sockets of her eyes.

At Carduelis it's not uncommon to hear words, random words, words the staff will call 'inappropriate', 'bizarre', 'freaky', 'gonzo.' Such words, now escaping Pola's net, scatter in some heedless place behind Cora and the passive male psych-tech for whom Cora finds fervent, body-brushing, orientation needs.

Words. The usual indecipherable, random garbage of words, only words: 'faceless face', 'bloody hands,' 'crashing, crashing, crashing door,' ' snake drinking there,' 'emptiness, emptiness, emptiness.' Sensible only as cracks in the matrix of the indecipherable, and nothing more. Just words.

Except to Pola, who was alone again. Alone with Johnny: Seeing, seeing, seeing — his compass of the Forest speaking: its languages of stone and branch. (Janivik had once proposed a description of Pola's language, wanting to explain it to Romi: He called it *articulate speechlessness*).

And this is now. And this is real. And this.... is breaking her heart. Seeing, seeing, seeing. Always seeing:

In the valley of the pines. Green branches torn from trees. So neatly piled in this long file of tepees, each branch a fallen soldier. How it must be to see the war —the endless war— that way. So neatly stacked, the green-bough tepees. So long this file that runs beyond the hill. Where does it begin? Where does it end? Each branch a severed child from what great tree. Your heart is darkly finding, your feet are darkly moving, your eyes are darkly searching. Far away – the hooded stone. So without motion. Seated there. The master, leading monster. Its bandaged hands so bloody, dry and bloody.

So hard to look into its face, its hooded face! And Johnny, Johnny, don't! Oh god, there is no face! The dark — the empty, empty, emptiness —

○

Cora notices the absence of Pola and begins to casually search about. In the dining room, which in the evening becomes the recreation room, several mental health refugees considered to be in transition to a civil life are seated, wordlessly gazing at the empty ping pong table. Doreen, a timid nurse-trainee, is explaining to Mary Louise that she can't smoke here, and then discovers that Mary Louise is using the hot end of her cigarette to scorch her own flesh, because she so much wants to 'feel something,' Doreen will later be told. Gantz, a sullen faced and youthful giant, once known for tearing a steel door off its hinges at the Human Services Center, sits docilely at one of the dining tables holding an uncut deck of cards and watching Doreen, wondering if he can ask her why his good eye has developed this persistent tick and can she fix it. Gantz's other eye is gone, his having ripped it out of its socket sometime ago. It was to Janivik that he explained the Old Testament requirement, 'if thine eye offends thee, cast it out.' Gantz was haunted by obsessions of the kind he tried to explain that day: "I kept looking out the back window of our car at girls in shorts, and then the green hedge mentors would come. They are always out there to punish me." When Nurse Doreen told Gantz his tick might go away, and it did, Gantz thereafter called Doreen, Santa Lucia.

But until they had discovered Pola was missing, the biggest interruption of the night was the distraught mother who came in with her fifteen-year-old son, Dempsey. The hyperactive Dempsey had been discharged only a few days before, but the Ritalin drugs Dr. Gass had sent with him had little effect on home life at the Triple Vee Ranch, twenty-two miles east of Cambria. "Even the cuttin' horses is goin' wild when he's out there," Dempsey's mom says. "I think we gotta take him back, try somethin' else!" Her words were near to a scream. That was when Cora returned to the room with a sudden rush to find her misplaced cellphone.

○

Seated in what looks like a construction site — raw beams hanging from rods, a row of tall, bare windows exposed beneath a vaulted ceiling — Janivik smiles at Romi, her seductively split kimono falling loose as she reaches across his lap to a lacquer bowl of seaweed crackers. Their wine glasses are almost empty, but before she puts the glass to her mouth again, she wags it toward the ceiling. "You know with all those grand windows we can't be far from the canals of Venice."

Janivik smiles again and tosses his chin toward the ceiling. "Are we working on a strategy of escape?"

"No strategy. It just happen," Romi says. "Strategy is indecent."

"Then, no strategy to bring good wine to me?"

"Mindful drinking is just that. No strategy."

○

At Carduelis, Pola enters the communal bathroom. The intensity of her vision has not changed, has not stopped seeing the 'empty, empty, nothingness, the void within the faceless hood.' Her shoulders are hunched, her chest seems caved. Yet her face, scans upward, her eyes searching every detail of this bright room. It is the bulb above the sink that finally holds her attention. She fills the sink with water. Steps in. Squats. Still looking at the light. Suddenly she shatters the bright bulb with her fist, and turns her mouth and bleeding hand toward the bare filaments like a desperate child seeking breast. The jolt is like a charge of darkness. There is no flame. Just emptiness. Emptiness. Not even the nourishment of death.

○

Talking. Touching. Sweet manoeuvres of nesting and seduction. The teasing hands of Romi and Janivik, still within their nineteenth century rendezvous. And that is when the telephone rings.

"Is this television," Janivik scowls. "They always answer, but I won't." Yet, what is this thought that worries him. He reaches to the phone but Romi, snug behind, holds the receiver down.

"First, this message:" In his ear, her tongue so loose and wild, so reeling in its shivered soft of gold. Yet Janivik, the reluctant stoic, raises the molded messenger and grunts his name.

"No! Damn it! No! I'm coming." Romi sees this pained hope for the hopeless Janivik look, and is suddenly out the door with him. "How can they," he moans. "Suicide — she's tried — "

○

At Carduelis, a corridor of staff and patients looks on with catty appraisal, or hidden delight as Romi passes with split garment and bare feet. Entering the infirmary tight behind Janivik, she hears someone whispering, "concubine."

Pola is alive. And when Janivik leans close to her bed he thinks he hears her speaking a confused, apologetic mantra through her bandaged lips. Her eyes open and softly shift with recognition as she speaks. "Johnny.... the emptiness, the emptiness, such emptiness, Johnny." Her eyes close. Her hand, bandaged and blood soaked, flops onto her chest. In that instant she has fallen into sleep.

Chapter Fourteen

The supervising psychiatrist at Carduelis is Doctor Oren Gass. He is, in his own perception, a radical independent. Janivik would not be at Carduelis if this were not so. Somewhere on the periphery, Gass had a kind of remembered curiosity about the experiment at Kingsley Hall, where Janivik had participated in a uniquely alternative community of psychotherapy, and when Janivik first met him, Gass had commented, "We could use a little radical thought like that around here."

But in the months that followed Janivik saw Gass more as a free wheeling administrator, a practitioner who enjoys the clever manipulation of patients through maneuvers of applied psychology. Pure conditioned-response, dog-psychology, Janivik called it, the same trickery that dominates the advertising industry, a talent, he told Romi, that would have made Gass a great sales exec, especially in the marketing of drugs. Gass's self concept as 'radical' come from his own experimental intuitions about how to influence behavior — tricks that were not necessarily even in the behaviorist lexicon. Controlling the patient, not discovering the patient. From the beginning it was easy to see that Carduelis was on a behaviorist path, but Janivik also saw some wayward bends in that path and wanted to be there, wanted as well to be near Romi.

When Janivik first came to interview at Carduelis, he had come into what had been called the Director's office and found a man in paint sopped rags, painting a pale pink onto the wall in an office with three freshly painted blue walls. When the painter asked if this was the Dr. Janivik he'd scheduled for an interview, Janivik had smiled, delighted that the potential boss-man had apparently abolished the role bound behavior expected of the director in a psychiatric care center. At Kingsley-Hall, eliminating all the artificial staff and patient roles of conventional psychiatry had been a step forward into a sense of equality and family, where the actuality of play meant more than the concept of rule and control.

Curiously, with Gass, Janivik became the listener and was asked almost no questions for the entire interview. "The color of these walls will inform, even influence client behavior," Gass explained. "The color of the sun room will be white, because that's the color of the sun. Like Newton's prism," Gass said, "all the colors of the spectrum are there in the white. But in black the whole world of color just gets sucked up. Don't get me wrong, I'm no fuzzy color therapist, but I have noted that color is emblematic of behavior. So much so that I find myself labeling them by color types. The orange ones, for example, are the really, the most unsettled, anxiety ridden ones. We won't use that color here anywhere, but the client may be that color. As you well know, you won't find that label in any book of psychiatric classifications, but this is how I work. In the real world of physics and behavior, you can't run orange through a prism and get the whole rainbow of colors like you can with white, you just get more orange. That is true with most of the cases we have here. If their color does not bend in that prism, they are either lost or we bend them some other way. Drugs have made that possible. Sometimes. For some, behavior transformation works a little. You know — Watson, Skinner and the others."

If you know a better way. Show me. You're hired. That was not exactly the total of it, nor did he say it that way, but that is how the simplicity, the eccentricity and the bluntness of the man struck Janivik. Other factors, Janivik's personal Zen meditation and commitments at the Gateless Gate, where he had recently met Romi were part of it. But the peculiar eccentricity of this maverick-behaving Dr. Gass suggested something of a tricksters-playground and Janivik, though he felt forewarned, was ready to see what he could do at Carduelis.

Chapter Fifteen

This morning Janivik must meet with Dr. Gass regarding Pola's attempted suicide.

And Janivik tries not to anticipate which Dr. Gass he will encounter: the trickster, the administrator, or the behaviorist. Though trying to see Dr. Gass for his audacious independence, a man who has so far supported Janivik's commitment to Pola, Janivik gets lost in appearances: Gass's eyes, like needles, a triangular face with a chin abrupt as the end of a football. Why the flat at the top of his head made Janivik think of a turnip field, he didn't know — maybe the short snags of hair that never quite come together on his balding pate.

But when Janivik comes into the office, it is the administrative Gass who outlines his 'the buck stops here' responsibility and says, " ... but we are here to take care of the patients, not to take them on trips. I want her back on chromopromizin, or was it haldol, or, or whatever it was before."

Janivik: "I can't."

"She's suicidal — violent — and is taking half the staff to keep her together."

"Yes. Yes, I agree. I agree, too, that this should not have happened. But. In my estimation, she has made extraordinary progress."

"I'm afraid each time you report progress some dark thing happens. No. I must request that you put her back on the regime, doctor."

"Dr. Gass, I have studies, experiences which show these drug programs only appear to help them while they are here. Patients who have not had drugs make a better recovery after they leave hospital care. We're operating a shelter – a little cubby-hole of escape, not a place of healing. Pola, like no patient I have seen in America, is in touch with the real resources of her health — which the drugs would be blocking!"

"Even if you were right, it would take every moment of every day to ... (he breaks off). Last night she would have died if the circuit breakers of this place hadn't been designed to protect patients like this. Do you want to live with her?"

"Yes. If that's what it takes.

"You have a — (he glances at an organizational chart on the wall) about twelve patients in your therapy. How do you accommodate them?"

"One at a time, when they are ready. Right now they have their prescriptions, and I meet them in group. Let me take Pola out of here."

"I can't recommend that."

"If her guardian requests it?"

"She's committed to us. We have to release her." Without subtlety Gass points to himself, "The word must come from this office. I can see the press release now: 'Psychiatrist at Carduelis takes female patient home to live with him.' Just the kind of good news we need."

"O.K. She can live with Romi."

Gass pauses to wonder, 'how naive or persistent can this Janivik be'— when the intercom on his desk interrupts:

Intercom: "Dr. Gass, Pola Fredericks is gone. We can't find her anyplace."

Janivik throws a defeated glance at Gass, who throws an angry, all knowing glance back. But Janivik is out the door, while Gass continues his response to the intercom. "Have you called security?"

Intercom: "What security."

"Alright. Get me the sheriff."

○

Janivik is at a stairway landing looking at a track of Haldol pills spilled along the steps. He runs to the top floor where he sees a ladder set to go through a ceiling hatch. A workman coming for the ladder sees Janivik disappear through the hatch. Unsure of what is happening, the man glances again at Janivik's disappearance and saunters patiently back to a tool box and bends —

Janivik, running along the edge of the roof, suddenly sees Pola crouched against an air-vent.

He slides into a squat against the parapet of the roof, close enough to be seen by Pola. They exchange silent glances, then Pola speaks. "Did you know it will soon be Christmas?"

Janivik: "What—?" He looks around at a swirl of white cottonwood tree fluff that is falling from the nearby trees and whisking along the surface of the roof almost like snow. Is she thinking snow, Christmas — "What—?"

Pola: "It's the last time I will ever see you Johnny. Christmas."

Janivik, fearful that this is a continuation of the suicide episode, tries to redirect. "Christmas is still far away, Pola."

Pola: "Not *this* Christmas, the Mystery Keeper Christmas. I know you were looking for it that day. The day they will shoot you." Janivik ponders her references to a Mystery Keeper again, something in the language that she and Johnny Valjonni shared. This time it comes with an urgency he hasn't heard. He wants to leap ahead and put this 'mystery thing' in place, but this is when the intrusive face of an orderly pops through the hatch calling back to someone below: "Here she is! We've got her."

○

Moments later, Janivik faces a stormy Dr. Gass coming into the hall from his office. "We had," Gass says, "My God, we had the sheriff going to every ranch house, every bush around here!" Janivik looks at Gass with silence and no hint of apology as Gass continues. "I regret this, but, Dr. Janivik I think she has been set up for this, and if this goes on she will have to go State. "She's full of deceit, she spits her meds, she won't —" He stops. "So it's intravenous or a padded cell."

"The pad then. I'm going to spend the night with her there."

Gass looks at Janivik for a very long second – *a marvel, a goddam stupid marvel* — "If that's your therapy—"

Gass leaves. And Janivik goes toward Pola's room. It is difficult for him to tell her about the padded cell. But the vine is quick at Carduelis, and Pola already knows.

Pola: "I don't mind. No doors — no drugs — no — no mistakes." They smile.

Chapter Sixteen

When Romi leaves the Sakura with three Styrofoam boxes of take-out and chopsticks, she pauses to grab some paper napkins, silly napkins she thinks– stamped with a fat and smiling Buddha.

She smiles at the prospect. Three people in a padded cell eating the osaka and the vegetable rolls.

○

In the pad-room at Carduelis — a converted office space lined with gym mats — Janivik and Pola are into a quiet-time looking, sometimes laughing together as they page through an old torn comic book with a picture of the Pink Panther and Clusoe on the cover. Janivik has determined that this first evening with Pola, Romi and himself in this strangely confining space will somehow be social, light, maybe even like a happy family experience. A place where anything goes, no probing, no reminders of recent events, in a way, even going back to the security of the crib, though he is not convinced that regression is at the crux of Pola's alignment needs. Playing with feces was going-back, but creating or experiencing mandalas could be constructive. A secure and healing connection. It's as though Pola is in some kind of dance, going back and forth. Back to where she was with Johnny; forth to where their haunting relationship with each other and the Forest wanted to go, but was so tragically severed. To where her obscure references to 'truth keepers 'and 'mystery keepers' are often at the bruising end-points of her dream stories. Except, they aren't dream stories for Pola. She holds these communications up-front, and presents them, albeit emotionally, as though she were an interpretor of another language.

Another language, something he feels unable to adequately explain to either Romi or Gass. Gass who had said, "You can collect her dreams for three-hundred years and she'll still be lost. Get them straight, give them shape, or they will travel on forever in that disconnected schizophrenic world," Gass advises. Gass with his bold biker's fantasy— a prejudicial trick of mind that Janivik knowingly allows himself after watching Gass rocket away on his 'Sturgis' emblazoned black Harley one Friday night — that fantasy of bold independence, of Gass imagining himself a pragmatic revolutionary in his use of color, space, grooming, drugs, yet all of it still within that systematic regime that reminds patients they are sick and we, the psychologists, are the healers. The behaviorist psychologists all have their mazes of slightly different shapes, but at the bottom Janivik is puzzled at their evangelical delight in being shapers.

Such treatment in the usual psychiatric sense does not alleviate suffering, rather it perpetuates it. This has been Janivik's conviction and experience since shortly after his first psychiatric residencies. And it was confirmed as he observed the recidivism in his next two residencies. Doctors only become social trustees attempting to maintain conventional behavior, he concluded. Trying to maintain conventional behavior by relegating patients to impaired roles is worse than putting blind children in blinders because they look blind. Emotional straitjacketing. That kind of psychiatry conceals the journey, tries to get people to forget what's bothering them rather than come to terms with it.

Because Janivik is not of what he calls the straitjacketing-convention his role at Carduelis is becoming, more and more, an attack on the staff's regimen and contributes to their distancing Janivik from the settled orientation at Carduelis.

"Another language" Janivik once blurted at a staff seminar: "Imagine, in America, that you were trying to communicate with the last member of an extinct Native American tribe, the last one to possess its distinct language and no other. Such persons, because we and no one else could share their language, have been committed and driven to suicidal desperation in our institutions. For Indians, this whole culture raps on that." The seminar went on to its next business, quietly treating Janivik's comment as eccentric, a mere show-stopping fluke.

But Johnny Valjonni, the blue-eyed Indian, was living on both sides of this cultural — this language — gap. And he was driven to both sides, Janivik guesses: the blond, Anglo-Saxon waif, Pola, on one side; and the intimidating fantasy of the Indian woman, Ramona, on the other side.

But is Pola speaking *his* language, *her* language, or some invented metaphor of *their* language. The point, Janivik thinks, is the urgency of letting her back onto this seemingly geographical terrain where *she*, or *they*, had been going when the event of Valjonni's death ended it.

○

When Romi is ushered into the cell with the take-out treats, she remembers Janivik's suggestion to be 'silly, lighthearted or something.' And in that sense of non-sense she slides the three plastic cartons around on the matted floor, offering them a choice in shell-game fashion, while sing-songing whatever comes out of her mouth: "Peter Piper picked a pad of pickled snackers... Pola take your choice it doesn't matter ..."

Pola isn't hungry, or won't eat, or feels inept with chopsticks. But the tea was 'dreamy' she said, "like the tea Johnny made from kinnikinick that one time we met in the forest." For Janivik this casual comment comes like a breakthrough. It was the first he could remember of Pola voluntarily clarifying Valjonni as her consort in the forest, and not himself — Janivik.

Romi finishes eating and wants to head off the awkward quiet she senses could be settling between them. She picks up Janivik's empty tea cup, and walks with her own empty cup toward the paper bag in the corner of the pad, but doesn't stop there. She continues to walk all around the perimeter, studying the walls as though she might find some muse there. Suddenly, she takes an oddly Kung Fu stance and kicks the padded wall with dramatic elegance, then quickly swings around with the cups, like challenging weapons in each hand, feet spread, hips centered in a low gravity stance. Pola's eyes are wide. Janivik laughs, stands as though expecting an invitation to dance, as Romi kicks the wall again and jump-spins toward Janivik, throwing the cups at him like knives in some metaphysical challenge. "This good four wall Kung Fu house," she declares. Janivik wades into the fray, cautiously ready to mock the challenge. Then, like a spring, he takes the spread stance, his two hands wheeling before him, palms out like a demented window-washer.

Parodying some old Kung Fu movie, Romi slashes forth, then stops.
Romi: "You cannot see, Master Po."
Janivik: "Fear is the only darkness."
Romi: "Do you hear the cockroach at your feet."

Janivik: "Do you hear your heartbeat." Janivik swings his head in a cobra rhythm.

Romi sallies forth with a full-breast charge, and Janivik does a reverse somersault on the floor, coming to his feet in a spread-leg defensive stance.

Still seated on the mat, Pola smiles and is coming alive with the oddity and the humor of it.

Romi: "Master Po, is it good to seek the past." She spins past Janivik catching his arm. They spin together.

Janivik: "Does it not rob the present." Their arms lock at the elbows, but Romi releases, and Janivik flies into the padded wall, turns and recovers with a valiant kick to the ceiling, which he remembers, as he lands nearly on his head, is how the laws of gravity, action and reaction work. Ready to cap the frolic, Janivik stays on the floor, huffing and laughing with the pleasure of their charade: "I think we not know Kunk Fook," he says with intention of ignorance, even of the form's name. He looks for Pola, and sees her indulging in a dippy backward somersault, then plopping out flat like both Janivik and Romi have done.

Pola: "Oh sleep! — Can I sleep?"

Romi looks up at the padded enclosure from her supine view, "What a marvelous bed — the world could turn upside down and, you'd never fall out." Pola sleeps and only wakes hours later when Janivik returns.

○

He notices she has saved the Fat Buddha napkin from last night's take-out snacks. It's worth a smile for both of them. "Lets go to the sun room for our morning visit and some breakfast goodies," he says. But Pola is silent, holds back.

"Can we do it here?"

This pad is some kind of a 'womb thing' for her Janivik thinks, or maybe from last night she thinks it's a playground. He wants her to get out of here. But. It's her choice. Soon they are stretched on the mat, looking at the ceiling, like mates in a kingdom-sized bed.

Something biographical was happening. She may have been telling Valjonni's story before, but now she was calling him Valjonni, at least for now – Valjonni on the streets of Cambria, Valjonni (or Johnny) in Aunt Kate's car:

"Aunt Kate saw him a lot at the bar. Said nobody could never get him to say much, except they could lush him for an easy beer on payday, then tease him for little things like never tyin' his shoes, or for runnin' stop lights with that old balloon-tire bike that the kids called his 'chopper' just to tease him when he rode by. Katie, she kinda looked out for him. She knew the war, the saws, his mom, his Indian strangeness was all runnin' up against him. Said he was always study'n things, odd things, like even that dark mole on her face, or like when she passed the jerky-jar to him – he would study it like maybe they was bugs or somethin' in it. He could study a thing, like a half dead fly spinnin' on the bar, like it was a sad, important thing, she said. But, I didn't know him then.

"The day he smashed his bicycle was the day I met him. And I didn't know about the bike then. Katie was driven', taking me back from the old Lodge, and there he was walking along the highway, no more bike. But when Kate stopped he wouldn't get in the car. Said he was gonna walk, I don't know for sure, where. Maybe to his mom's. But Kate asked about his bike and just kept talkin' to him til he got in. He tried to get in back, but it was loaded with bottle cases, so he had to get in front with me. When Katie told him who I was, he didn't say a thing. But, yeh. That's how we met. Funny, when he got outa the car he stuck a five-dollar bill on the seat— tried to pay for the ride. Kate got it back to him at the bar. But. That's how he is. (*'is'*? Janivik notes Pola's surprising present-tense reality shift.) Always tryin' to be so independent, I guess. Take care of himself, I guess."

"But how did you meet in the forest?"

"That was after he got outa Cambria. His new life. With a beard. It took him — a hard time to get out of Cambria. The helicopters and all. The town followed him. It came after him, like a Ghost Town, even in a place where he tried to sleep. Tried to sleep, but couldn't – the wind blew, rickety buildings rattled, and he said he saw strange policemen coming out of the walls. Their faces covered with sheets of metal, all of them the same. And each time he would almost fall asleep, they would slide out and raise their guns at him. So he had to go. Deep into the forest. He said it was his 'helpers,' sending him deep into the forest. Where he found the cave. The Ice Cave. That's where we really met. That's where he spent the months before we met. I was just ridin' by, me and Bet, my little white pony, like I used to do when my daddy was alive and ran the dude ranch out that way. In those days it was like my playhouse. But ...

"He was very long-faced. 'Specially that beard. I didn't know if he remembered me. From that time. In Kate's car. We were both kinda scared.

He didn't want to be discovered. But right there, near the entrance, at the big stump, that's where he saw me. That's where I always got off of Bet, cuz it was easier with the brace I used to wear on my leg. And suddenly, we were just lookin' at each other. We were both, like, intruders. He was in my old playhouse, where I used to hide and make funny noises when the dudes came by, and nobody knew. But now I was in his hidin' place, where nobody knew.

"I just said somethin' like, 'I use to play here. He kept sayin'I didn't know, I didn't know,' and I kept steppin' into it, the big cavern where it opens, not really scared anymore, because he was so sorry-actin', and timid. And how could he be scared of me — a little girl, kinda limpin' along. I wanted to see if he was really livin' in there. And he was. It was a sight! That ice cave is big. It could hold a house, and it was like a whole life in there. Things like dried berries, dried meat. I saw some arrows and a bow he made.

"I don't know why, but I picked up one of the arrows, examined it and kept it in my hands. In the back was the 'wikiup,' he called it, branches piled kinda like a tepee to make a cozy place. That's where I stayed sometimes. Many times. But then, but then — that time we met, that first time — he just kept sliding away from me. He didn't even smile when I told him about scaring the dudes, and how I would go back home to the lodge and listen to what the dudes would say about the things they heard. But he smiled when I said, 'people are scarier than ghosts, and how daddy would get angry and say, 'You could get shot doin' that.'"

"Anyway, it was the kinnikinick berries that made us both laugh. There was this big can of berries right near where his feet were. So to say something, I asked him. Asked him what they were. And he said, 'kinnikinick.' 'Kinnikinick —' it made me want to laugh. Then all the sudden, he gave me a fistful, and put another fistful in his mouth — to show me how to eat 'em. 'Like Russian peanuts.' he said, 'only inside out.' And, flooy! The seeds just came flying out of his mouth. And then I ate them, and seeds came flying out of my mouth. And he did some more. And I did some more. It made us both laugh. Spitting seeds, like — flooy! And then a chipmunk came along and ate the ones we dropped. 'My chipmunks eat 'em too,' he said. He called 'em *his chipmunks*. That's when I knew he might like me too."

Janivik rolls over and squats on his heels. Pola raises on one elbow.

"But why do you call it the Ice Cave?" Janivik asks.

"Oh! The Ice-Angel! It's like a giant tree of ice in there, in the middle of this big cavern. A stalagmite, my daddy called it. It stands like in the middle of a pool, a black mirror of water. And water keeps drippin' down, and Her wings and Her faces keep changin'. Yeh, and Her drippin', drippin', drippin', can take you — anywhere — Yeh, the Ice Angel —" Pola draws down into a drifting slowness, sinks back onto her left shoulder, away from Janivik. Is on her side, looking at no ocular thing.

Janivik waits through a long silence. She needs to sleep, he thinks, and leaves.

Chapter Seventeen

Still on the gym pad and unaware of Janivik's departure, Pola reaches back to the tenderness she felt in that first meeting with Valjonni. Her words have fallen under the hypnotic spell of the dripping water from the arm of the Ice Angel. And yet under the quilted voice of memory, she sees him, oh, so clearly.

At the Ice Cave, Pola, still holding the arrow, stands behind Johnny Valjonni, his bearded face and struggling eyes gaze painfully out of the cave, into the forest. Him saying ... " but I'll be leavin' now."

Pola asking, "Because of me? I won't tell, Johnny. Not even Kate. Kate said she hoped you'd make it." This hunted man in a cave of ice. I wasn't huntin' him, but he was hunted. I wasn't hunting him, but I was finding him. From that moment I began to hear in that *other* way, his words that made no sense at all — but sounded like the voice of something lost.

Pola: "You must get very hungry."

Johnny: "... course I get hungry. I get very hungry sometimes. But hunger. It's... It's like the wind. It blows though me like the wind. And feeds me. The *hunger* feeds me."

"I wanted to be the wind. I wanted to know what he was saying." I handed the arrow to Johnny. I watched him, wishing he would say something as I walked away. Only thing I said was, "Johnny, please don't go.

"I didn't ride Bet that time. I just grabbed her rein and found our path into the trees. When I looked back, I saw him still standing in that scattery light, still holding the arrow in his hand."

Pola looks back, expecting that Johnny is still in that "scattery light." Or was she telling this to Janivik. But what she sees is the canvas wall of her empty padded cell.

Chapter Eighteen

In Cambria, even months after Johnny Valjonni was killed, the explanations — the what and where of his fugitive life — still simmered in and out of their bleak closets.

There had been a posthumous court trial, and the mark of negligence ascribed to the sheriff's posse by the judge might have had some healing effect on the town. But that was also the season for the U.S. senatorial campaign, and the local candidate, Bill Burch, wanting to show himself clearly on the side of law and order, restated again that Valjonni's death was "justifiable homicide." The state legislature, also lobbied by the Peace Officers Association, endorsed Burch's view by declining a judge's request for family compensation.

For Sheriff Don Blaine, Valjonni was considered armed and dangerous. And his six months as a fugitive would make him hardened and hard to catch, even with the eighteen man posse he was organizing.

For the sawyer, Bert Garretty, who had twice talked to Johnny in the forest, Johnny was 'no way dangerous or armed.' And when Bert saw another posse moving out, he'd cursed Blaine and made his own offer to bring Johnny in: "Let me find him Blaine! Sheriff, you don't know the man if you're goin' out there with all them guns! Let me find him! God damn, all he did is pee in your goddam streets!" But Bert had also been part of the cactus-in-the-butt taunt that let it out how Blaine's first posse hunt for Valjonni had recklessly careened an unannounced gas bomb into the backwoods shack of a single mom and her two screaming kids — transients up from Arkansas, ready to start a new life, but, as Bert told it at Kate's, 'they left so scared they didn't leave word or trace.'

At the Towner Coffee Cup, Mary Anne Goss, with her tight blue perm, and Selma Dean with her leather necktie and tooled purse, had their own speculations about this figure they had only seen from across the street.

'Lurking,' was the word they favored. "Never know what he might do if he finds some little girl out there," Selma said. Because of some recently rumored incident in the school, the chatter moves up and down the counter. Butch, from Butches Standard Oil — a former Seal or Ranger, and quietly known as a genius of back-country survival — speculates that it would still be tough to live out there alone for all this time. "No problem," Selma says, "there's been a lot of break-ins lately." Next to Butch, and finishing the last dregs of his coffee, Slim Berglund, a barber comb in the pocket of his clean white jacket, pauses to trim the palaver before he leaves: "I knew Johnny long before this happened. He never hurt nobody. Just came home a little crazy with that 'ganistan shell-shock stuff. Nobody talks about — he got a Presidential Citation."

The deer, elk, goat and mountain lion hunting seasons have just opened. And the four-wheelers, with their tide of sagging carcases aboard, are on the street with the show-and-tell of early morning. Also at the Towner two aliens from Ohio, big game rifles visible in the window of their parked truck, are paying for the 'hunters special.' The one waiting for his check tries speaking to the mood of the place by catching Mary Anne's guardant eye. "Sounds like a fugitive loose 'round here."

Mary Anne: "Shot at some kids in the school the other night. See some kook in the woods out there — better shoot first and ask questions later." Mordantly processing her grim thought, the man reaches under his mantle of florescent orange to his wallet of credit cards, scratches the ticket, and quietly tools his way to the door.

Chapter Nineteen

Johnny's mother, famed rodeo acrobat and trick rope performer, Rita Victory (her stage name) had been told by the Veterans Hospital service officer, when Johnny left Ft. Belvedere, that she should take a guardian's responsibility, that he would need social support, some kind of job stability and for her to be make sure that Johnny take his pills.

Not ready to classify him with a post traumatic stress disorder, a diagnosis not yet clearly defined in Veterans Medical Centers at that time, he had been classified as a 'paranoid schizophrenic,' and should he show signs of "acting out," — things — they qualified — as public disturbances, suicidal behavior, alcoholism, even refusal to take the prescribed anti-psychotic drugs — then Rita might need to arrange some time for Johnny at Fort Belvedere's psychiatric ward again.

Rita could testify to the drugs. She was using them. Their tranquilizing benefits were, she told Johnny, what 'keeps me apart from the hard things — building the arena, raising money for the rodeo, worrying about you.' Rita's glamor as an international rodeo queen, performing in such places as Madison Square Garden, Las Vegas and the Denver Stock Show, went a long way in this little mountain village of Cambria which foresaw a glittering tourist attraction in the offing now that Rita Victory was committed to a permanent venue in her old home town. Rodeo entrepreneurs, bored dentists, and even a venture capitalist from Pueblo were joining in the fun and party times of raising a little money for Rita's Arena Project.

Rita 's personal vision always came down like a hailstorm of agendas for anyone in the snare of her lair. Racing with her feet on the top of two horses while roping a pistol packing clown "takes a Houdini" she would tell her crew of wranglers, performers and backup attendants.

These days, Johnny, would one day be expected to haul the manure from the barn and the next day run some promotional photos up to Wild Horses Multimedia in Colorado Springs. But, if and when the big show happened, Johnny's role was well planned. He would be the Wrangler, and the only one allowed to touch her horses, like his dad, the one they called Old Chauncey Valjonni or sometimes just 'The Indian,' who, on cue, at show-time, donned the role of a clownish, drunken, pistol packing lunatic running loose out of the grandstand, so Rita could heroically lasso him in front of a hooting crowd.

But Chauncey Valjonni had run away from it all. Completely disappeared. And now Rita was discovering that Johnny was maybe starting to balk, not going to let her groom him for that role. Being a ward of Rita's wallowing grandeur, and still buzzing the big logs at Cambria Sawmill sometimes made him feel eerily like he was the log and not the sawyer. Then one day, when the V.A. prescription came in the mail, he tried the pills again. That was the day he lost all traction with the big lever that brought the massive saw-teeth down on the constant chain of logs as they entered the mill. The next day the Cambria mill foreman had Johnny sign for his last check.

It was also the night he shared his final check with the usual free-loaders at Kate's. And the night he stepped out of the alley at the wrong time, just after the Deputy's patrol car had been chained to the bridge abutment and two gamely pranksters were doing cookie-spins around and around the intersection in their long black Impala, simultaneously screaming rebel calls out the window, and tossing noise-maker beer cans to the pavement. It was a damn good joke, Valjonni thought, especially when he knew the Deputy had been asleep in that patrol car. But after the rubber-smoke and exhaust settled, Valjonni had jumped down from the piece of construction scaffolding that had been his viewing perch and landed, unwittingly, into the emerging faces of two errant pedestrians of the dark night, frightening himself and the pedestrians, who, within minutes, hailed the sheriff's car with uncertain tales of harassment and identity.

Chapter Twenty

Sheriff Blaine didn't come to the house to talk to Valjonni about these incidents. He talked to Rita.

"Messing with a patrol car? Chasing people down alleys? What is this?" Rita asked Johnny as she suddenly appeared in the door frame of his room.

He hadn't thought 'til this moment that he would be identified as the car-chaining prankster. But while Rita ragged him again about taking his V.A. pills, he remembered the two arm-in-arm strangers he'd practically bumped into that night. In that same blink she was holding the pill bottle in front of his face. "If you took 'em, these things wouldn't happen to you," she was saying.

"I took 'em and it did. Why don't Blaine ask me about what happened? It's me! It's me! Me! You think I'm crazy, don't you — that's why   why?"

○

Within a few days after Johnny was laid off from the mill job, Rita abruptly entered the sagging plywood partition that had become Johnny's bedroom.

Naked, except for his jockey shorts, his leg stretches to the sill of a small window from his seat on the edge of a disheveled cot. With a blue pen he is doodling an obscure image onto his bare thigh. Mildly bug-eyed, Rita pauses, letting the odd tattoo or perhaps the weirdness of the act momentarily erase the message she has come to bring him. A new job she'd found for him. The job is at 'Sanator', a long-defunct tuberculosis sanitarium recently converted to a place where 'feeble minded' is still the reference given to inmates by the folks in Cambria. A fearful place, in Johnny's mind. "No way, no way, no way!" he screams at Rita. And Rita screams back:

"If you'd just work, they'd think you was okay," And "besides it's an outside job," she emphasized.

Chapter Twenty-one

And it was, sort of, outside. Window washing. But on his second day, fixing his ladder to a third floor window he saw something that withered him into a near catatonic free-fall. What he had seen, he had tried not to see. But they were still there when he looked back. He was seeing into a ward of mongolian deviates. A child he could not escape was thrusting a spastic, contorted claw toward him. He saw then that it was not a child at all, but a waxen faced underdeveloped man in bulging diapers. Caged on its back in a high barred crib it grunts hog-like. Its hands, tirelessly flexing, pick at the air.

When Valjonni looked down on the rungs of his ladder, he heard without words the gravest most destructive question – saw the cretin child and the question merge and follow, heard its voice again in the far-off rip-saws of the mill. The scream of fate. The scream of idiocy. One scream.

He began to slide, but his jacket caught onto a joint of the ladder. Then mercifully it tore free sending his feet skudding stumplike against the rungs to the bottom. He ran across the lawn to his bike and rode blindly into the village, while the saws of Cambria mill whined and amplified a cretinous projection on the window of his grey sky.

In Cambria he ducked his eye below the horizon and careened wildly across lanes of screeching traffic, bounced over the curb through a covey of pedestrians and down to the corner where Don Blaine's patrol car suddenly blocked his way and sent Valjonni skidding flatly on his hip and across the gutter. His bike was half under Blaine's bumper when he looked up from the bruising crash and saw the stern faced sheriff talking down at him. "What the hell kind a crazy thing you doin' here! I'm gonna have-ta take that bike plumb way from ya." But Blaine's speech began to falter as he watched Valjonni stand and raise the bike threateningly above his head, then, in the same instant saw him hurl the bike viciously against the concrete walk and jump wildly up and down on it, smashing its spokes, trampling and flogging it into a mangled ruin.

The sagging Valjonni looked back at Blaine and with astonishing anguish cried, "Take it!" Then he looked away, and not quite leaving, he turned mournfully back to Blaine. This time the same words were from another voice, softly, softly collecting his whole misery: "Take it."

Touched by the anguished sadness in his voice, the little crowd that had gathered slowly parted, and Blaine turned mutely to his car.

Chapter Twenty-two

Valjonni on his derelict bike — his grey almost ghostlike passage through the streets was how Norton, the stonemason, remembered Johnny, except for those times when Johnny came to help Norton move and cut stone at Norton's carving studio. There he was a strong, dependable but intractably silent partner. It seemed his voice could only be used for important, or maybe unanswerable things like: 'why should we cut such a beautiful stone.'

It was on the rocky grade of a road that came back to the highway near his carving studio where Norton saw some trucks and a hearse bump up from the ditch, actually saw blood running from the back door of the hearse. "There was a kind of edgy banter, even laughter, when I heard them talking. Like from some big hunting party. But a hearse? I hadn't been there when they crossed my land going in. And then I saw the sheriff.

"I followed them. They went to the funeral parlor, the morgue. I had to see what I was too stunned to believe. Told Colin, the undertaker, I was his only brother, and he let me in. They shot him in the back! I touched him. Saw the place where the bullet entered. Put my hand in it. They shot him in the back! They shot him in the back!

"I'm the one who went after that god damned posse, made them come to court. Couple others joined me, paid the bill: Richardson, you know – owns the mill, Comanche the sculptor. It was an odd lookin' court room. All the — couple dozen — spit-and- polish police officers, Highway Patrol and such over on one side. On the other side just the three of us plus Carrie Lee — coverin' for the Chronicle, and Humpback Joe, the village jaw-harp-poet."

Chapter Twenty-three

Cambria lets Johnny Valjonni die.

Pola does not.

For Pola, Valjonni remains the presence of anguish, instruction and mystery.

For Janivik, Pola's stories continue to come like messengers. Messengers of healing from that strange Forest of Experience she so mysteriously divines. Whether they are inventions of hers or Valjonni's, they are endlessly new, remarkably telling. And Janivik encourages her every expression. Twenty-six months go by, and even Dr. Gass acknowledges improvement, no longer demands the old surveillance. Gass is actually intrigued when he learns that Pola is using her water paints on the windows of the sun room, staring at the sun, making fierce rainbow balls of fire, one of them with something that looks like the shadow of an eagle slicing through the clouds. He has also heard the speculation from staff and clients that her crazy talk is getting crazier: That she has now contrived a story about 'how she lived with an eagle or was he a man who could be an eagle.' Some of the clients like to hear these stories which Pola sometimes tells when she paints. Some of the clients know they are 'lies' Cora says, and 'some actually believe them.' When Janivik heard Pola's 'eagle story,' Pola began it as a simple hike or climb to the top of a tall granite pinnacle to see an eagle-nest with Johnny. Seeing baby eagles and then fleeing when the parent eagles soared and threatened down on them. "It was on our way down from the rock that he stopped to look back up at the soaring eagles: I still think it's strange, but I loved how or what he said anyway. He looked at the eagles for the longest time. Then he said, "Sometimes I think I been there. One day I slept at Keepers Mountain and dreamed I was an eagle. And when I woke up, I wasn't sure I was a man who saw an eagle or an eagle who saw a man."

Discussing the tale with Gass, Janivik called it the ancient Lao Tze butterfly myth. What an old friend from the Laing experience might have called '*ecology of the mind*,' the compelling innocence of knowing you are the *other*, even as the *other* is you.

"Ecology of the mind?" Gass smiles.

Janivik smiles too, "Yes, 'far out' as they used to say. But, what if enough people thought like that, would we still be poisoning the animals we eat, the air we breathe?"

Chapter Twenty-four

One Saturday afternoon Romi brought Janivik back to the Gateless Gate, the Meditation Center where Janivik and Romi had first met, where Romi still meditates and teaches with the dharma prisoner meditation groups which come there each week. A group of monks from the Tibetan Buddhist monastery of Drepung Loseling in India will be doing a mandala painting there. And, Romi wonders, 'would that be a way to better understand Pola's strange mandalas, or if they are, indeed, mandalas at all?'

It is not the first formal mandala construction either of them has seen, but both Romi and Janivik view the event as a moment of spiritual reckoning. Of acknowledging the universal and cosmic implications of mandala paintings and their occurrence from the micro to the macro in nature, in science, and in cultures throughout the world. But today both Romi and Janivik feel a compelling involvement relating to the personal and seemingly naive constructions of Pola.

○

The Tibetan Buddhists have crushed, ground and prepared colored sands from the colored stones they have found in Colorado. And today, before they begin the actual construction of what will be the intricate sand painting, a chorus of monks, their heads festooned in saffron roaches and shoulders draped in maroon and Crocus sativus robes sing a tantric chant (though the monks have said they are words) in sounds which resonate from a deep auditory root.

For both Romi and Janivik, the sounds and sights of this day fall into a wave of exploratory meditation, blessed with questions, even silent conversations.

He holds the thought: Sounds that resonate from a deep auditory root, sound which Janivik feels is utterly centered in the cave of primal sound, itself. What can I possibly mean by such words Janivik asks himself. I mean, like some primal stone rolling through the darkness of a great cave, rolling toward the light. That for me is mandala sound. Unlike voices elsewhere in the world, the Tibetan Chants are multiphonic, in one voice intoning the three notes of a chord. These monks have saved something from the ripple of earth's first fusion. But how? Where did they go to extract this essence and convert it to communication? For her part of this answer, Romi remembers a dharma meditation, a realization that 'where there is no audience, there is no mandala.' She actually remembers the monk, who had said, 'no audience, no mandala.' Is this why Pola creates these image/stories, because she has Janivik for an audience. No, Janivik has said: she does it alone, too. In her strange removal, she is the audience, the audience for Valjonni, and we are outsiders looking on. Or if we are recognizing some of her images as mandalas, it is because mandalas are inescapably in our bones, too.

Many hours go by in witness of the Tibetan sand painters. Each monk draws intricate lines of sand. Each line seeps from tiny funnels onto lines that have been prepared with an earlier chalk drawing, a cosmic drawing of inward and outward motifs. In this Tibetan painting their are traditional symbols that have traversed the ages as ritual and conceptual mantras. Learned mantras reprising and echoing in the hand of the maker, and demanding perfection. In this aspect Janivik finds Pola's spontaneity nothing of the same. He thinks she has taken the comfort zone of the mandala as an originator, a maker, an artist discovering a natural and inescapable cosmic artifact, or, again, that her Valjonni has done this, somehow through the mind of his art, introducing it into her psyche. From Pola, the revelations have come to Janivik as actual moments in time. Here, the monks are not sharing a sudden revelation, they are sharing an incredible living history, a kind of 'timeless time,' but in outward respects, a re-recording.

When the Tibetans finish their encyclopedia of the finite and the infinite, as it has been described for them, they sweep the sands into a jar and the audience follows them in a procession that leads to a tributary of the Arkansas River, where the sands are emptied. The cycle of life written in sand and water.

Chapter Twenty-five

Driving home that night, Romi had commented, "Going to the Center, the way those mandalas were painted, it's, in its way, all about shelter, isn't it." Janivik nodded, but both Romi and Janivik remained quietly with their own thoughts on the drive, a kind of peacefulness holding them there. Romi's thoughts returned to how she had used — what she would now call a modern mandala form — images of architect Buckminster Fuller's Geodesic Dome — in the dharma meditation. The ultimate balance of structure, all of its parts contributing equally to the whole. It was, or is, a real world architectural dream, a concretely obtainable and livable space, mathematically pure or consistent. Yet, in its purity, there is such reduplicate simplicity that it may only ignite a sterile challenge to imagination. Compared to the Buddhist mandalas and a mandala like the Taj Mahal, with all their inexplicable dance of color, space, mystery and polarity, makes the 'geodesic' seem singular and aesthetically colorless, Romi thinks.

To Janivik, Romi said, "Those Tibetan monks, though they used words, which I didn't understand, and chants, and music, and that marvelous sand painting, it seemed that the communal heart of what they did was that visual thing, the mandala, its shape, its journey from the sand, through all their hands and to the river. The whole action was mandala, but the memory that holds is in my eye, is at the center of the center — that visual moment."

"Yes, for me, too," Janivik says. "I think language is not the first big thing in primal memory. If I could imagine the world before, 'In the beginning was the *word*', as they say, I would have to believe that language is only a substitute for vision. For me real communication has to acknowledge *vision*, those things we *see* that can inaugurate intuition, an intuition that can read and create metaphor. All of this we have seen today is history, or tradition. It is very confirming history, but it more than suggests that we are not personally living in that place. It suggests to me that to be alive we must always be creating that place. I don't know what effect seeing this mandala demonstration would have had for Pola. The Tibetans were repeating something. She is at the creative edge of finding something. Her language is unique. And I see transformation in the images she presents. I think hers is the same personalized mandala experience that the amazingly articulate psychologist, Carl Jung wrote about. He acknowledged mandalas like, you know, the great cathedral windows of Chartres for their universal congruence with nature, but he also built his own personal mandalas. After his wife and mother died Jung built a house for himself. A round stone tower with a fire place at the center. He said he saw it as a kind of a maternal womb, which gave him a feeling that he was being reborn in stone. He built, he said, as though he were in a kind of dream, but afterward all of it fitted together into a symbol of psychic wholeness where he said he felt himself spread out over the landscape and living in every tree. He also painted other mandalas on the walls there. Called them 'the exponent of all paths, the path to the center.' These mandalas, he said, took him to a place he called 'individuation'. Which for me, looking at the word, would be the opposite of the divided self."

Romi shrugs her shoulders. "So what you are telling me is that Pola is working or making images just like in your Dr. Jung story. But. What about this individuation thing? I think you are also telling me she hasn't gotten there."

"She's not Dr. Jung," Janivik says, "And I'm not Dr. Jung. I am just looking and listening and talking in this bumbling way, wanting to strike a chord. And hitting the wrong chord so often is getting to be an awful noise." Janivik turns in a gesture of discouragement but sees in the intensity of Romi's eyes that this should not be the end of their conversation.

Janivik's long, obstinate pause is not enough to stop the question in Romi's smile. "When I take this up it's like babble you know. Words," Janivik says. "The point is: our limits of perception, my limits of perception, the tools we have, our conscious knowledge, logic itself cannot go to these places. I think we find in these mandalas the *unconscious* knowledge. But we still have our divided selves: the *conscious* and the *unconscious*. It seems like human kind is in a battle to keep them from ever communicating, when instead we should be finding how to bring them together. Some of the people anthropologists call primitive, or I would just rather call human-kind from a remote culture have found a way of reckoning with these two selves. The Bush people of New Guinea. Some of these people have what they call a *"bush soul."* Maybe it is in that same sense, that Pola said Valjonni talked about having a *helper*. Those "bush-soul-people"can have a helper, a mystical participation with their bush soul. That psyche or soul could, for them, even be a tree, or a crocodile, a dead grandmother, and they might wear a mask of that image, a crocodile for example, that confirms this connection, perhaps eliminates the division. I could also imagine Pola having Valjonni as that mask. It is a very strong thing. A man with a crocodile-soul can swim safely with crocodiles."

Romi's smile is ambiguously facetious and searching: "You could be talking 'drama,' 'art,' 'dreaming.' But connecting with an animal, a dead grandmother? What is the connection? I mean, what, really is it? Telepathy, clairvoyance? I've heard your guy, your Dr. Jung, had what I'd call telepathic experiences. Visions of things happening in extraordinary synchronicity, reaching into other places and times from where he might have been standing. I think he called them something like the 'sympathy of all things.'"

"What is it —?" Janivik re-asserts the question, "It has to be 'All of the Above.' 'Us in Nature.'" He stops the car in front of the big glass doors of the place they call home before he continues: "Yeah, why not call it an ecology, an ecology that really is *all* those things. A mystical participation that lets our *mind* — call it 'our psyche' — *in* with the rest of nature — *one thing*, instead of being divided into two things: *us* and the *environment*." Janivik pauses, looks across the room unconsciously at a book shelf. "You know, my greatest mentor, who could explain this stuff, even to psychiatrists, called it a "Sacred Unity."

Romi smiles, "Sweet name. Still it's intellectual, not the real '*ding*.' Like in Zen when deep calls to deep, or the visual image: 'A brightly burnished mirror facing another brightly burnished mirror with nothing between.'" Romi wanders to the table with the smooth round rock she loves to touch when she talks with Janivik. "It's the flat-out communication some of this suggests that staggers me, Pola with Valjonni." Romi squints blankly at Janivik. "So you think Pola has gotten to the place where she is *in with nature?*" Romi asks. "And you think that explains her seeming mystical communication?"

"I think when she is in that Valjonni Place, she might be touching the underside of it somehow. But what the drugs, the psychiatrists, and her education, mine included, have done is teach schizophrenia. So we get stuck. Darwin, Descartes, Newton, and too many other great explorers have co-opted us with schizophrenia.

"If Descartes had said 'I commune therefor I am,' instead of 'I think, therefor I am,' maybe some of the scientists and others would have stopped observing the world as a 'logic' called, 'me and *it.*' '*It*' as all this cause and effect assumption stuff outside of us, outside our little thought-engaging neurology, that separate thing, we still call our mind. It's that mold which predicts the double-bind, predicts schizophrenia. Schizophrenia, even if you could kill it with a drug, is still schizophrenia. It's the double-bind that addicts us to war. What we have usually been calling schizophrenia is double-bind, and double-bind is a chaotic rewind so complex, that, if you entered it into a computer, it would wear the computer into a heap of junk with its constant expressions of double-bind. Again, not so different from the question of the Sphinx: To the mother the Sphinx says: You can Answer, Yes or No: 'will I return your child'?. If the mom says 'yes' and the answer is 'no', the child will not be returned. If she says 'no', then of course already the child will not be returned. It is a no win double-bind. In a double-bind there is no right answer. In double-bind we torture each other, we torture humanity, we torture nature to get the answers we want. But it takes a relationship or a collusion to perpetrate. And the collusion of the Western World with its webs of classification and its superlative 'cause and effect' successes have trapped us. Even the 'yes, no, yes, no ... of our computers can only produce product. It knows nothing of *process. How we really make an image, really make love, really see each other.*

"We have taught our way into madness, and we won't find our way out with the same teachers." Janivik stops, shakes his head and sluffs his shoulders apologetically. "God, it's not you who needs to hear this." Janivik steps away and plunges himself firmly onto the couch.

Romi shakes her head with a smile. When Janivik sees *this* Romi, this calm and forbearing muse, he cannot name the kind of beauty she is to him. He can only take it to some place in childhood, when he saw the calm blue depth of a flax field in morning sun.

In the quiet, Romi moves to a dark-doored cooler hidden in a nook across the room, rustles a block of pale cheese but pauses before she does anything with it. "What you call double-bind," she says, "is written all over Valjonni's war with Cambria. Even that useless little gun he pointed at himself was still a threat to the posse. Just being a blue-eyed Indian was enough, but the riddle he was being asked was one he seemed to be asking too, when he said, 'stop or I will kill myself.' Talk about 'collusion.' Yet, what was the child, this mystery, he was protecting. Was it a thing or a process. Is it Pola's child or his?"

Chapter Twenty-six

The tincture, not the detail, of her inner world was becoming most of what Janivik experienced of the newer, evolving Pola. But that was enough, Janivik thought. When they had their regular visits in the 'Room of the Broken Horse,' the transcendent muses of Valjonni were still apparent, and seldom repetitious. To dig into their world was becoming unnecessary voyeurism he was beginning to think, especially now that Pola was 'talking to the sun' with her water paints in the sun room. These images and her descriptions of them were the most extraordinary expressions of her pain and her recovery — the two sides of her balance-wheel. Yet, like a mother in the throes of birthing, the anxiety traveled forward with her. What was this 'child' going to be? The Mystery Keeper, she still talked about was as abstruse as the Holy Grail. She won't get there. But the journey going? Is that enough? The shoals of her journey — or Valjonni's — Janivik knows well enough, have driven her close to suicide and have the nasty encroachments of something out of Dante's Inferno, or Bunyan's Pilgrims Progress. She is too fragile. So is our ability to guide her too fragile. Yet she is navigating in this world of the psyche, as though some real Psyche might at some point present Herself. 'I cannot navigate in the radar of her psyche', Janivik reminds himself. 'And what goes on, goes on'.

Chapter Twenty-seven

Johnny Valjonni

It is autumn and Valjonni is dredging the wet clay from around the pool of the Ice Cave. He takes the clay to a knoll near a ridge above the cave. Past a circular pile of hot stones a wood fire burns, heating more stones for the clay-burning. Fragile clay figures — figures Valjonni has hesitantly called his 'Truth Keepers' when he must define them for Pola— are postured round-about on the rocks and nooks of the ridge.

For Pola the peculiar knobs and heads and animal shapes are more like Johnny's playthings, things they sometimes laugh and smile about. Some are masks and, once when Pola had looked away, Johnny had even slipped a mask over his face and startled her.

One is the 'Faceless Hooded Figure' now draped with fetishes: porcupine claws, jawbones, feathers, pieces of antler and even an old purple medicine bottle looped around the cavity of its hood. Another is an eroded mantle of a beggar's face, its hand stretched upward into the shape of a cross. At the very top of the knoll a crone-like mother-of-the-world figure sits weaving a robe from which a strand of sinew stretches into a little mud-faced coyote's mouth. Pola knows the story. Haltingly, Johnny had once told Pola how, with his daddy at a Lakota Sundance, one of the 'old-ones' told about a Woman at the top of the world. "That Old-Woman," he said, "is weavin' a robe, but each time she goes to stir the stew in her pot, the little coyote unravels the quills of porcupine she's weavin'. That Woman and that Coyote are always doin' this," Johnny said, "and if she ever finishes that robe it will be the end of the world." After a long pause, with Pola studying the primitive clay, Johnny said, "That's the way they talk out there."

Only one other time was there even the briefest explanation of the figures. That was when Pola asked about the enigmatic smile of a broad-faced shape near the bottom of the trail. "That's 'Laughing Water,'" he said. "He laughs 'cause he knows the wind will have him." Then Johnny looked up at the stony spires shadowing the ridge from behind, "... and the rocks don't know. The rocks don't know," he repeated. Pola could say nothing. Too crazy she thought. Then, at Carduelis she thought again. But that was the kind of talk that always got her in trouble with the shrinks, she reminded herself. For Johnny she could imagine the clay and the wind dancing and disappearing. That's the way Johnny thinks, connecting natural things to natural things. The stone, she imagined, wasn't so ready to dance, or at least was so stiff against the wind that it would be hard for it to know the 'wind' would have it too.

Explanations were not what Johnny could give. The clay figures, the wind, or, whatever, had to be their own explanation. Not like things, but between things: "That's where all our relatives are talkin," Johnny said. For Pola it was like you could have a hand with fingers, but what made the fingers talk was the space of emptiness between the fingers.

Chapter Twenty-eight

At Carduelis

The primitive grace of the eroding clay affects her. Pola feels awakened when she sees them. But now only in her mind's eye.

From her minds eye Pola rubs the many colors of clay onto the side windows of the sun room. With a soup spoon from the dinning room — they wouldn't let her have a knife — she spreads in feverish palette-knife-like strokes, tinctures from the tubes of moist water paints. Ochres, siennas, sands and umbers; shadow-greys and sepia. Then, with erasure tips and finger tips she lets the sun come through in traceries of bold cartoon. The Old Quilling Woman on Top of the World in one abstraction; Laughing Water in the sweetness of another; Absurd Birds and Horned Beasts whose tilted elements suggest unanswered questions from the jagged ridge lines of the forest.

Three weeks before, when Dr. Gass first saw the dimming, clay-like diffusion on the windows of the sun room, he was nearly apoplectic. Then, as he spun to vent the gall of his discovery, he saw Pola's first sketch of the playful, tugging coyote puppy, the sun catching its edge-lines with aurorean gold. Exhaling in a breath of befuddlement, his mutterings could be deciphered as: "Amazing. The spectrum. Amazing." Exiting the room, something turns him back. Squinting for an angled view of the coyote pup, he takes the cell phone camera from its holster and clicks. Bends closer. Then clicks again.

But for Pola, the clay figures, the storytellers that Johnny had stammeringly sometimes called his 'truth keepers' were still like desperate infants searching for something on the other side of blindness. If it was there — that thing that haunted him — she wanted to touch it. Perhaps on the other side of death.

Chapter Twenty-nine

Johnny Valjonni

"Death, knowin' death is there, that makes me 'live'" he had said that day she brought him the birthday cake for the make-believe birthday party. "I already been born, the birthday's over. Death's the most important thing now." It made Pola sad. That kind of strangeness vaulted Pola into the realization that Johnny wanted to be near the edge of death, like that night of his storm-dance, with all that lightning slamming on to the tower. He could have cowered and run away. Instead, he joined it, and it changed him. Or sneaking through Cambria at night for food from the school cafeteria kitchen, then, at midnight, going upstairs to the gym where the drums were, and beating his madness out on the drums, until some boys heard him. When those two boys found courage enough to turn the gym lights on, Johnny was flat behind the piano, invisible. And the two boys were spooked, seeing nothing but the empty, lighted gym and solitary drums, where only seconds before there had been a booming wildness of drums beating out of darkness. They did not wait to explore the ghostly absence. In solemn-faced slowness they retreated, until, in Johnny's reckless exit, the drums crashed loudly against the floor and sent the boys running in panic certainty that guns were firing close behind.

From Kate, who heard everything that happened in Cambria, Pola heard one part of that story. From Johnny, she heard another part of the story. When it was all put together, the story made Johnny's eyes look shrewd and gleeful.

It troubled Pola that Johnny did these things. He was even letting himself become a mystery voice, sometimes casting the curdling sound of a coyote — half pup, half hyena— in the hearing range of sawyers and miners in the forest. It was a sound that had invented itself that night after the tower storm, when he had watched the sturdy, pony-faced girl with the long yellow hair dance naked in the glass walled cabin of the tower. Johnny, hiding on the roof the of the tower, had been suddenly shaken by the 'rockamongous' sound of music bursting from below, and found her dancing in seductive, stripper-twists to a row of muscle-magazine-cover-boys propped along the sill in front of her. Reflections of her enormous breasts frolicked in triplicate along the glass walls. For Johnny, his long hair dangling from the eaves in his upside-down view, it was a trick to stay concealed. When she turned his way, he dodged quickly and sat in the darkness as the music went on. He could smell the seductive sweat of her body. He wanted her. He hated her. She was on exhibit to the world and to no one, a fantasy in a glass box.

A shroud of frigidity filtered around Valjonni as he thought of the girl and thought of his mother, the rodeo exhibitionist, twirling her rope from the back of a prancing white horse, feasting on her own reflection in those eyes of the thousands. His mind sickened. He hated this girl. He might even kill her if he should touch her.

The dancing stopped, but he could see her nude body in a reflection from the slanted open window. She was eroticizing herself. Then the music stopped. On the horizon a broad silent flash of heat lightning opened the sky.

Valjonni began crying – began laughing. Hysterically he laughed. He dropped from the roof, to the rail, to the stair. He was overwhelmed by a sadness, a love, for the girl, even for his mother – a forgiving painful lonesome love. He could not touch them, and he was running.

An hysterical laughter barked through the forest. And on the tower— the lonesome, pony-face girl stood screaming.

○

From the light and dark of those two nights on the tower Valjonni knew something had changed.

Chapter Thirty

Johnny Valjonni

The fresh pitch of new-cut pine trees spiced the air and ripened with the whitening hues of morning sun. After months of wandering in the forest, Valjonni's legs began to move with an urgency. He bounced across the tops of three granite knobs, swung lightly from a branch to a cat-like landing on the bridge of a felled tree, gyroed to its root, then pounced again into a tree-shunting slalom among the lesser pines. The blackness of the forest had been swept away and the the green needles prickled with silver light at the infinite blue. Even the groaning of a woodcutter's chainsaw was song.

Valjonni vaulted over another cut log and anchored himself abruptly to the view on the slope below. A sawyer was walking to a marked tree, his idling chain purring in anticipation. At the base of another tree, closer to Valjonni, were the sawyer's gas can, his lunch pail and a grey parka.

The thought of food sent Valjonni dashing after the lunch pail, but just as he made it to the tree the sawyer looked back and yelled, "Hey!" In that same moment Valjonni seized the parka and was running deer-footed into the forest. When he heard the sawyer call his name, Valjonni wondered, then remembered that the sawyer was a man he had seen many times, usually at Kate's.

The sawyer chased and called after Valjonni, but the uphill run was too much, and he finally returned to his saw. When Valjonni stopped running, he settled into a pile of springy branches, and looking at the grey parka still in his hand, he wondered why his hand had taken the parka before the food. And he thought about the pleasure of being recognized – of being pursued — yet being free.

Those two times the sheriff had almost found him had made his life in the forest even sweeter.

Now Valjonni regretted having to leave the fire tower so soon. He had thought of a cunning plan to bring the sheriff out after him again. Perhaps there would be another chance at the tower: He would call on the radio grid: "This is Valjonni. I'm at Cicero Lookout. Tell Sheriff Blaine I've got a gun, and if he wants to bring me in — come ahead."

Valjonni nestled more securely into the brush and fantasized the sheriff arriving at the tower with a posse of dozens picked from the streets of Cambria. Valjonni saw himself hidden in a tree watching as the posse surrounded the tower and yelled for him to come down, or be shot. When they got no answer, he saw the sheriff firing a tear gas bomb through the open door, and then another one. No one coming out. Who would go up the tower-ladder after the 'mad' Valjonni? He wanted to be sitting in that tree just above the sheriff when they decided.

They would probably fire some more tear gas bombs and leave, but Johnny hoped for more bravery than that. He wanted to see the lone brave man go up the tower and the thankfully-spared-posse spread out on the slope to cover with their telescopic rifles. Valjonni, who had seen both the panic and the courage of soldiers sent to take a sniper nest, saw this man coming in panic, firing wildly through the deck as he came to the hatch. Yet from his tree near the posse, Valjonni knew he would soon be laughing, could hardly wait.

That was when the brave-posse-man would see a coat oozing red where bullet holes had torn through it. A coat, with a hat sagging from its collar — stuffed with blankets and a few cans of tomato juice here and there. He could hear the brave man yell, "It's goddam trick! I'll kill the bastard!"

Valjonni would wait, and watch the whole posse climb the tower to see the ruse. Then he saw himself jumping out of the tree, laughing his hyena-coyote call, and running all the way to the ice cave. There were no roads and it would be dark.

The fantasy. The plan was so alive in his head that when Valjonni leaped from the bed of branches near the sawyer's whining saw, even the sawyer heard Valjonni's curdling cry.

When Valjonni entered the ice cave he pulled the grey hooded parka over his head and felt the empty monk's cloak of it fill and nourish him like the skin of a new man.

In the back of the cavern Valjonni slept to a metronome of water dripping from the tip of an enormous ice stalagmite. In winter the phallic stem must have grown nearly to the roof in its endless baptism. Now in summer it was melting, through a kind of tinkling conversion, into a many faceted ice angel. That night Pola came to lay down beside him. She came so quietly he did not know she was there. And yet he had dreamed she was there, that she had come on a horse whose head was the 'Four-Faces-of-Three' like the ancient root he had seen the day of the snake. He was so haunted by this that they did not make love. Instead Valjonni walked to the entrance of the cavern, needing to see the horse, yet knowing it could only be a dream. How could Pola bring the Mystery Keeper to him? How could he bring it to her? It was about that. It went both ways. It was for her he had to find it. It was for him she had to see it.

He had decided it was gone, never even there, something that might have hallucinated in his head that day. But always as he walked along the rocky cliffs above the streams that rushed as always through the forest, he searched. It was so real, this 'heart,' this 'grandmother,' this 'soul keeper,' this 'face of death.' Its face like a stone that grew from root and held such mystery no words could tell. There was no way he could create that face in clay. He didn't dare. He wouldn't try. And yet he muddled.

O

Rifle blasts littered the forest as the season for slaughtering the deer and elk came again. Hearts, livers and heads with tongues discarded by the hunters became Johnny's food. He was able to eat, slice and smoke abundantly without ever hunting. But there was a mood of violation about the forest as florescent-coated hunters ground into every trail of the timber with their Blazers, Broncos, Scouts and Explorers, spilling bottles, shells, firing and wasting.

It was near the end of day. Pola had returned to Cambria and Janivik was feeling a great solitude. The low light of the western sky was casting through the cavern entrance. It gave him the best light for muddling in the wet clay, or for getting lost in the hypnotic dripping of the ever-changing ice-angel. He was sketching the lumps of clay with his favorite tool, the hard smooth point of a deer antler, when, like some kind of target practice, he heard what seemed to be two rifles in steady intermittent blasts. So close he feared he'd have to run again. Run into the naked light and disappear. But there, in the path of his exit he saw the desecration — the shards of clay, his truthkeepers were tumbling from the ridge above. Running upward against the falling pieces of broken clay, he made it to the ridge while the deer riflers were still pummeling his peopled mountain. Bullets were still skidding white scars in the stone where he had come to stand. He could not remember what hopeless, angry thing he screamed at them. But something he did, some gesture of his helpless arms, still held in memory — still held in the veins of his open arms. Was it the offering of himself. Or was it the beginning of *knowing*. Knowing: He wanted to *choose his hunter*.

○

What Pola saw when she returned was a new darkness, and Pola saw it everywhere. In places where she could not be.

When Valjonni limped numbly back down the slope that day, an invasion, a strange soul of revenge soiled his heart and led him back into the forest and out onto its peripheries where other invaders, homesteaders, hardrockers, clearcutters, had commanded the forest to retreat.

The memory of Cambria revived in him, and he was returned to the fear of those first days after his escape from jail. He revisited the crumbling ghost-town where a fitfully slamming door had chased his sleep and spooked him away with hallucinations of State Troopers in cold steel masks. Disbelieving their reality didn't help. In that separate reality he had begun to see that his visions were more real than flesh. Now he was asking to return through that same fitful door of madness. The message for him then was to leave. But now he was returning.

The next afternoon he entered a deserted ranch house whose outbuildings were collapsing and torn apart by wind.

His mind retreated into injury. There, inside that boarded house, an aura of dementia confounded him and fluttered along its flaking walls, assaulting him against another wound.

Compulsively he searched through barren shelves and tiny closets, over stacks of yellowing magazines and moldy fruit jars. He frisked the pockets of some dingy overalls, then crossed into a second room where wads of stuffing from overturned furniture spilled out of musty vermin nests onto crazes of broken glass scattered along the floor and across the flatness of a disembodied clock face.

Dust spilled from the cover of a Watchtower pamphlet as his hands scoured the surfaces for some artifact of response.

Then, in the heavy drawer of the Watchtower-table, he found a cigar box packed with a miser's cache of gun debris. Cylinders wheels, trigger parts, firing pins and bullets of every size. A devil's stash of homeless parts. But scoring in the bottom of it all, a cunning, ravish gleam blurred like false diamonds in Valjonni's sight. A derringer. A tiny, sudden — weapon.

Like precious metal Valjonni seized the tiny pistol and held it. But its trigger fell back into the box, and when he retrieved it, he could not make it fit into the mechanism again. He rummaged the box for bullets that would fit, but each one he tried was too large. A witless diabolic satisfaction seized him as he grasped a rude fist of bullets and glutted them into his jacket pocket along with the trigger and the impotent little derringer. It was ended. However diabolic, the search was ended. He turned and saw for the first time across the room.

The end of the room was a cell, a tiny room partitioned by long vertical timbers, prison bars, which only allowed forbidding slots of light to pass between them. A steel mesh door with a massive padlock on its hasp sagged open at one side. Valjonni reached behind the door to examine an object of leather straps and rings. But in the instant of his touching, a sudden terrifying repulsion jarred him. *Manacles!* He let them fall like stones of fire.

Perversely, against that barrier of repulsion, he entered the cell, someway, somehow, to imagine — like a death wish — the enormity of idiocy, the enormity of madness in manacles. To play a dreadful game. To, himself, wear the mantle. The twisted wire door fell shut behind him, and like a clairvoyant he tested each bare relic: a steel bed-frame, a chipped enamel bedpan, a large kitchen spoon, a battered metal plate which held flockings of asbestos from the rotted ceiling; and then in a moment of ghoulish identification he lowered his eyes into a horizontal slot which must have been the food trough. Through it he saw the sagging trinket drawer of the Watchtower table. A sickening voltage lashed against his head and charged him with the traceries of this afflicted haunt. He ran out into the deep snow. Followed by a child.

It was *the child* or non-child that followed him that day from Sanator, the *child* whose thrusting fingers could turn the siren of the saws. The *child* Valjonni carried on his hip.

From that day, six months had passed — seasons out of time — Valjonni riding on a fatal spiral. There was no way he could go back, and no way he could endure against the enfolding premonition. *The feather of an unseen bird eddied along the surface of the snow, and behind it Valjonni saw tiny beads of frozen blood.*

From the drops of blood, he followed the etchings of frantic wings and claws in the crusted snow and found the frozen bird itself, at the end of its desperate arc. The red shell of a shotgun had been ejected a short distance away, and the large flat tracks of homo sapien trailed back from the shell to a road.

Valjonni flew with the bird, saw its panic, the death beat of its wings; and in that same moment his vision became detached, and he was seeing from above, through the branches of a dead birch tree: himself and the bird, his trail and the pitiful arc, the red shell and the oblique tracks of the hunter.

Chapter Thirty-one

Carduelis

At Carduelis Pola had stopped casting the clay figures on the windows of the sun room. Her trauma of their remembered destruction above the ice-cave darkened her. She felt saddened that she should have the figures on the bright windows and Johnny did not. After the hunters had destroyed Johnny's clay people on the ridge above the cave, she could only remember his darkness. How, as she now told Janivik, "Johnny was like a little animal running in the shadow of an eagle, challenging the sky, challenging *The Hunter* "The Hunter," she repeated. "Saying he wanted to *Choose His Hunter*."

○

Now Valjonni's darkness is Pola's darkness as she walks wearily into the sun room this day.

Three of the clients, Molly, Fran and Boyd, are playing Chinese Checkers on a folding banquet table near the door. Gordon, the balding, comfortably round psych-tech who has been at Carduelis for years picks up a stray sweater from the back of a cushioned chair and wanders toward the hallway. When he acknowledges Pola she doesn't respond, causing Gordon no unusual blink of concern.

Pola glares at the encompassing mural of clay figures she has created over the previous months. Today, the windows are covered with slowly melting ice from last night's winter storm. In the light of the cloud-dense sky, the figures appear dark and colorless. Pacing along the sills of the first windows, the ones with the Old Woman Weaver and the Coyote Puppy, Pola mumbles grimly, but no one listens. In her head Johnny's story goes round and round: '... If she ever finishes, it would be the end of the world.'

"Right! End of the world!" she shouts, "End of the world — right!" She grabs a steel chair and swings it with great force against the window. It shatters and the people from the table jump up, but do nothing. Pola shatters the next window and the next until, at last, Gordon arrives and with Boyd they grasp awkwardly to restrain her. But she holds the chair against them for a shield, and when Boyd pulls the chair from her grip, she flies backward into the window through the shards of broken glass and Boyd lands backward on the floor, the chair on top of him as Pola spins wildly in this crucible of shattered glass ready to make the leap. But for her foot, held firmly in Gordon's grip, she would be on the ground below. Instead she is motionless on the floor of the sun room surging arterial blood from her right arm and may die if the ambulance doesn't make it through the snow.

○

The ambulance does not make it through the snow. It is somewhere cross-tracked on a downward slope, and a logging truck, unable to stop, has jackknifed and buried it under a load of logs. The drivers and their radios have barely survived, and the road is blocked "like Hoover Dam," the late arriving patrolman advises a dispatcher.

○

At Carduelis Janivik and Cora are stuffing tampons in the largest wound and feverishly pressure pointing for Pola's brachial artery just behind the big muscle of her upper arm. Oxygen is drifting into a mask on her chalk-pale face, but blood is still leaking, like from a massive battlefield wound, Janivik realizes, and he calls for a helicopter to come from the infantry combat center near-by at Fort Carson. It's like a shrapnel wound he tells them, she has bleeding wounds everywhere.

○

The helicopter medics have been to Iraq and talk distractions about everything but Pola — explosions at a check point, saving a child at a Baghdad shopping market, and about the jackknifed logging truck they had seen on the fly-over. Massive wounds are their business and in seconds the two medics apply sponges from a pack with a commercial tag stitched to it— 'QuikClot Hemostatic Agent.' Pola might once again recover, if, as Janivik hoped, she could somehow re-mold the better angels of that connection she held with Valjonni. But Janivik's hope retreats: she has just destroyed her better angles.

Chapter Thirty-two

Pola was a cartoonish patchwork of bandages but, amazingly, she could even joke about that when they began to talk again. It was dawning on Janivik that, for whatever else it was, Pola's rampage against her figures on the windows was cathartic.

But it was near the time of Christmas, so close to the time of Johnny's death that Janivik wondered if he should tread carefully with her, or try to charge ahead into what might be a crisis of revelation. Almost from the beginning some mystery from that season would burst up into her storytelling and get lost again. Even in July when the cottonwood fuzz was floating, it had happened. Some trauma or event before Valjonni's death had to be returned to, or re-lived, Janivik believes. Pola, he is certain, is desperately asking to find this place. Pola's smashing of the figures on the windows was as much a reviving, a reliving of the reality of what had happened to Valjonni and herself as it was a suicidal gesture. That day, above the Ice Cave, when the clay figures were blown apart by the hunters was, in Pola's telling, the day when Valjonni began saying that thing about *choosing his hunter*. Somehow Pola has chosen to find his 'hunter' too. Or is it her hunter, he muses. "This is where I think she is going," Janivik tells Romi, "And I am hearing an urgency in her voice."

○

There is a cold wind blowing from the sun room and Janivik notices a team of carpenters repairing the windows as he passes the double-door entrance and turns down the stairway toward the foyer. His view up the hallway is of a woman he doesn't recognize — probably a volunteer- hanging frosted-red bobbles on the branch of an evergreen. Relieved to see Janivik, the woman's eye turns nervously toward a suspiciously rocking shadow casting to the wall from the bright Pepsi sign on the soft drink cooler. The shadow is Pola's. Pola anchored and searching the way he had seen lost children in shopping malls.

○

It was not that day, but another when they got down to the wavering panic of Pola's Christmas. In the Room of the Broken Horse Janivik casually shows her some of the "toys" he has on his cluttered shelf. When he comes to the slotted-wooden-drum he taps out something with one of its super-ball mallets — three notes, three times, a cutely rhythm which traces each time like the phrase of a question. "I got this toy as a Christmas present once. I love it," Janivik says.

When he repeats the open-ended drum phrase, Pola's mouth opens, as though to taste some unbidden fruit. And in a suddenness her smile dawns like something behind the first breath of childhood. Slyly she is reaching, even laughing, as she takes the other mallet, and this time, hits the drum herself with a careless, resounding *fourth* note.

Janivik is stunned, charmed, grateful, for what he could not then say. Only that he wanted to embrace Pola in a way that he knew he would not.

○

Pola remembers bringing a plum pudding from Kate's freezer and asking Johnny if he knew it would soon be Christmas. She tells this to Janivik — how "Johnny kinda giggled and shook it off." But now what Janivik hears in her every statement is a question. Not the mythic stories anymore. Questions. "And what I got," Pola continued, "was all that 'Forest Talk' that threw me into mystery, his mystery I guess? How can I tell you? No way."

"Like what talk," Janivik asks. "Was he talking to you, or to himself."

"I think just Forest Talk. The words? The words: Like what did he mean, 'find his hunter?' He just said things I still want to understand. Like he almost screamed and said, ''I'm not look'n for no virgin, virgin thing!' Then he looked for the longest time into that pool beneath the Ice Angel. And when he finally stood up, the way he cocked his head, it was like he heard somethin'. I didn't ever think it was crazy but it scared me. Then he went back to Cambria. Like he always did — to dare some dark thing. Maybe it was Christmas or even the Virgin Mary he was daring. But how could that be? He just did things. It made me creepy to see him go that time. I think it made him creepy too."

When in his mind Janivik plays that questing voice of Pola's over and over, he hears a tragic-normalcy. She is out of the Forest and can't go back.

Chapter Thirty-three

Johnny Valjonni

This time he was walking toward Cambria. A perverse nostalgia begged him to see once again the lights and decorations of Christmas, and the silver water tower was the sort of station of contemplation that suited Valjonni's need.

As he climbed the ladder to the sloping canopy of the tank, he listened to the faint sounds of Christmas music playing for the early evening shoppers from a church spire: "O little town of Bethlehem ... above thy deep and dreamless sleep ... above the deep and dreamless sleep ..."

White flakes began to fall softly through the darkness, and Valjonni gazed hypnotically into a vertiginous dream of himself floating downward into the slowly turning vortex of snow. In this his heels slid loosely from the top rung of the ladder, and only the coarse threads of his jeans held him from the dreamy oblivion below. It felt so free to trust in nothing — to exhilarate in a power that was neither control nor command.

In the wedding of his sadness and freedom, the sickness of his nostalgia became a dead light, and the shock of its disappearance convulsed his body into hysterical laughter — which may have frightened the villagers below, in the idiocy of dreamless sleep, in the carnival of his black Christmas.

Dazedly he returned to the rungs of the ladder and joined the earth. He walked past shop windows and crossed Main Street in the glare of scanning headlights, yet no one recognized him, nor did he care. Once he stopped near the window of a brick house and watched a family of three decorate a tree, but like a man from another planet, he saw it happen and that was all. It no longer belonged to him. There was no gift in this. Yet in these moments a new polarity of giving began to grow in him like a sacramental curse.

From the fringes of the village he wandered outward into the night, and in the dazzling light of morning his parka like a grey monk's cloak was a vestment of snow. He floated in the delicious rhythm of timeless movement — his body going onward and onward. The fresh snow opened silently to every step. Every step was its own abstraction of whiteness, every step drew the blinding whiteness into the bleeding redness of his brain—purging him with feverish crisis.

From a veiled knoll of rock a virginal cloak of snow swirled in a capricious updraft. Valjonni stopped and watched in hard amazement as it became absolute form. It was Pola, or some messenger of Pola, standing on that wispy spire of stone. Her delicate body completely naked beneath the white transparency of her gown. In her hand she offered a bleeding chunk of red meat toward Valjonni. Continuously the meat issued from her hand, fell, and replenished in a miraculous flow. Never did her hand or gown become tainted with the dripping blood.

Then, 'midst a growing whine of saws, the virgin birthing died and broken trees of twisted crosses bent like beggars waiting to be green again. From behind Valjonni felt a growing menace of grinding, piercing decibels. He crushed his hands against his ears and turned to confront what he knew would be the changeling-cretin— child. Its fingers picked at the sterile air and disappeared. Then—

Endlessly walking out of a vast and eroded landscape, a form of derelict proportions came toward him, its hand held high with some emblem as one who marched alone in a religious pageant.

As the figure transcended the space between, Valjonni saw that it was carrying nothing in its hand, save the peculiar form of its sex-finger, elongated and fused into a fleshly cross. A watery self-pity squinted from the crimson lids of its jaundiced eyes. The grey face was tufted with ureal strands of hair, and behind its tusks of sunken mandible, its spastic tongue fluttered perversely, wanting to speak, but unable. Valjonni saw that the figure's clothes were identical to his own, and saw, in shock, the figure was a debasement of himself, its eunuch voice projected in solicit martyrdom, crying out: "I have suffered so much for my people— yet they will not crucify me."

With suddenness Valjonni's own cry pierced the air with anguish as he fell upon the Martyr-Man— himself flaying wildly in the snow, until in exhaustion Valjonni lay alone in a deep coma of peace.

From an injured hand, Valjonni's blood began to melt through the snow — tapping from the earth a distant voice— a ceaseless, changeless gallop.

Three times a red horse appeared before him, and when it appeared the fourth time, its black left foreleg thrashed at the earth and disappeared.

And Valjonni was standing— conscious and alive beyond ever having lived. On his shoulder he held the 'Root,' the 'Mystery Keeper,' 'The Four in Three.'

The Great Grandmother, the Unsearchable One, was riding on his shoulder, above the grey monk's hood of Valjonni.

Valjonni stopped. He gazed into the snow-patched forest of leafless aspen. He was sure he had seen something red. But there was nothing — only the leafless branches and the snow. He had gone no more than nine steps when the certainty of a red horse standing deep in the woods halted him again. But there was nothing for his eyes to see. As he tracked on through the snow, the question of the red horse moved in him like an ancient memory. Once more it happened and then it left him. This was Valjonni walking. A new man moving in the Forest.

There might have been triumphant music drumming through his heart as he strode with defining rhythm toward the Cave. Something certain and irrevocable had happened in the secret but forgotten co-mingling

At last the gift for Pola was clear. But he could not think of it as a gift from him. On hastening steps his spirit exhilarated. Would Pola be there when he returned to the cave? He would put the Root on an altar of Kinnikinick. For Pola he would not call it "The Four in Three," he would call it 'The Old One,' or maybe the 'Grandmother-Grandmother.' He still had time to think about that.

Through the white branches the dark entrance of the cave appeared like a Gothic window. There was warmth inside, and a new underground-suite played into the Angel's pool of melting ice. He placed the "Four-in-Three" on a ledge at the back of the cave and turned to imagine Pola coming through the door.

○

Something metallic bounced along the rocky floor, and the muffled pop of a shotgun echoed outside the cave. White smoke was rising from a spot on the floor. Its acrid mist was filling the cave and burning his eyes. Valjonni found his jacket and held it to his face as he ran by a second exploding cannister of gas.

He ran out of the cave and toward the dense woods from which he had just come. But a man with a rifle and a white cowboy hat raced at him headlong. Valjonni reversed and a gray-coated figure moved from behind a tree. He turned again and two troopers in helmets and gold badges came racing side-by-side down the hill to cut him off.

Valjonni circled and darted in animal panic, but the man with the white hat was gaining on him again. Valjonni turned to the creek and splashed waist deep through its icy waters, only to see another trooper rise out of the brush on the other side. Desperately he switched back along the edge of the stream and crossed again below. Then, as he stumbled up the bank he discovered the little derringer in his jacket pocket. And heard their voices:

"A gun. A gun. He's got a gun!"

The Trooper from the other side yelled at him to stop and fired a warning into the air. Like a curse, Valjonni screamed, "What for!"— then stopped with his back against an enormous tree. Another shot splayed bark against his shoulder and sent Valjonni sprinting from the tree.

Then, with almost prayer-like hands, he raised the little derringer toward his face, and sent the anguish of his voice back into the forest: "Leave me alone or I'll kill myself!"

A bullet entered his back, leaving again from the cavity of his lungs. Valjonni fell. From a broken artery, surges of red fanned a warm blossom into the snow. Stopped. And turned to ice.

○

No one has seen the white horse with Pola seated on its back, until her sudden and persistent scream is heard above the solemnizing silence of men reckoning with the deed of death, wandering toward the motionless body, a posse searching for rectitude, a way to wash their hands of this. But Pola, they have not heard till now —

And now, they turn to see this distant child limping through the snow, a white pony tailing like a question from the shadows.

And now, it's Bert. He comes too late to stop the posse, but sees Pola and her horse, and comes to them. The three of them in grieving.

Chapter Thirty-four

When Janivik enters the tall glass foyer doors of their home, he finds Romi with a hacksaw in her hand, half through with her project to create a letter H from the letter B, the bronze digit she has taken off the brick walls of their bank building. (Their home will then be the 'ankh', they once joked about, and not the place they still call 'bank' each time they speak of where they live.) She holds to the saw, even as they hug, and points with it to her work table. "I'm doing it."

With an implicit need to speak of what he has heard from Pola today, Janivik, nevertheless, holds his words and absorbs Romi's artful transition of the letter. "Ah! You said you were going to do it. From the den of lucre," he quips, "comes the tool of god. You are a sculptor," Janivik smiles. Romi is pleased to have him say this, but she knows it is an interlude to something else that is pacing across his face.

"I don't know." Janivik says, I feel crazy. Like bloody, bloody — I don't know — I can't get them outa my head; these trickster tales she so innocently spouts. They come like questions, and prophecies, and damn it they're getting into my dreams.

"Wait," Romi says, "This is Pola."

"Yeah, Pola." Janivik walks in for a closer look at the letter Romi has just crafted, but he speaks of Pola's latest language images.

"She tells me about a bird, a frozen bird. I guess, a kind of wounded grouse whose wings have left the trace of a desperate struggle in the snow. The frozen drops of blood. A red shotgun shell and the tracks of a hunter walking away. Even the branches of dead aspen trees. Somehow, Johnny seeing it all from above. And I ask her, 'Did Johnny tell you about the bird, when he came back?' And she says, 'He didn't *tell* me. I *saw* the bird.'

'When?,' I ask. '*Now!* she says. *Now!*' So, I say, it's your bird then. She says, 'It's *johnny's* bird.'"

Romi's smile is slow. "She puts you out there in a kind of time-warp doesn't she ... like something that has to have already happened, but is happening now."

"It's like that, but it wants to go further, and it can't," Janivik says. "She always goes to something around Christmas. About him walking in the snow. About the thing she sometimes calls the Mystery Keeper or the Hunter. And this thing is always a question. She hasn't seen it, wants to see it, is afraid of seeing it —" A Sphinx, an absolute Sphinx. And that's why I think she needs to get there. Not getting there is where I think her suicidal depression starts. It's like she is building a mysterious mandala that needs Valjonni or something from the forest at its center, and of course Valjonni is not there. And I think she has quit playing games to keep me in her story. She talks and talks about him walking in the snow, but to where? She never gets there. She sighs, shakes her head, and gives up."

"A Sphinx," Romi asks.

"That's really how I see this in my head. Sounds odd I know. Yeah, Sphinx. The word is so filled with ancient myth that no one uses it anymore. But I like it. Some things are timeless and just keep connecting. And connecting is what I have to think this is about. The Sphinx talks metaphor, is metaphor, and that is Pola's world. In Pola's world of images is where the mystery train travels. If it is made to travel in the world of logic it will crash. I know it sounds like fairy tale stuff — Greek myth, but, damn it, the basics don't change. Our personal images of the basics may change: What was a horse in my grandfather's dream might be a motorcycle in mine. It could be any old puzzle-master we'd invent, but the Sphinx-Tune sings like a *round*. It's been here, it goes there, it comes back. Something we could take back to the future. Not just some one-way road. So: The Sphinx, however the Sphinx is shaped, is at the summit of a life or death journey. And however She is shaped She challenges those who must enter the city of new gods with Her questions. In mythology she dies or kills herself if the question is answered. But if this is Pola, it's not being answered. And finding the answer to the Sphinx question has always been the scariest thing, because the real question is in the logic-illogic of 'double-bind' and can't be answered without Pola becoming another creature, or a creature unbounded by isolate reason. In ancient mythology, it could be made into a death defying riddle: 'You must give me your beating heart, then answer, yes or no, if I will give it back.'"

Romi's shoulders almost leap to intervene. "My god, Janivik, it sounds like Pola is already unbounded from reason, and besides who is there to ask this death-defying question. This old jargon is not quite working for me."

"Well," Janivik hesitates, "The 'death-defying' Sphinx is more into ancient drama, or into primal trickster tales, but the psychology stays right-on and is spiritually timeless. And we know the only ogre who can ask that question is the ogre in Pola. Obviously I am with Pola trying to ask that question too. But what you said: 'Pola, already unbounded by reason?' This is where she has made all her healing moments happen. She is still working, which makes me feel like the Ogre's is still haunting her. In her dream-scape, isolated from reason, I see her wanting to cross that fear-barrier into her centering mandala creations. But if her Johnny Valjonni, or Valjonni's Hunter, or Valjonni's mysterious hallucination, which ever it is, is at the center of her quest it's going to be hard. She now knows he's dead. What makes me a little more hopeful is that she is no longer displacing Valjonni with me."

"Okay, maybe I can collude with you," Romi ventures, "in the sense that you are unraveling knots and we are both seeing Pola capable of vaulting through the inadequacy of logic toward some kind of enlightenment. This is all Zen for me: the paradox of the koan. For Pola, I can only imagine that she is in some painful place, 'of being afraid of herself: being afraid — of being afraid.' Your kind of double-bind knot. So, if she's on the Mountain, what's the next *illogical thing*? That question between her and the Sphinx?"

Janivik laughs, "The hypothetical *logic* of the *illogic?* I don't think it works. Are you teasing me?"

"No, you know I don't tease you," Romi smiles. "But I hate playing out the hypothetical. That's why I use the Koans because they are never hypothetical; they are everywhere in Nature, and that is what it comes to — everywhere in Nature. Like in real Nature, the answer is already in the question: 'Is the mountain high enough? Is the ocean large enough? Thankfully we can't measure that. So that's why I like it so much with those Buddhists on the hill. We go there never knowing if the gateless gate is a gate, but we go there."

"That's your journey, Romi," Janivik says, "and I love it, but the Pola-with-Johnny journey is unique. I thought I was somehow guiding her, but I'm not. With Johnny she is in that pain-place, where I can't go. And more likely she is guiding me. She has a clear vision of something, something I can vaguely dream about." Something I think I do dream about," he suddenly confesses, "Does that put it outside of time? I don't know, but that's why

I brought the Sphinx in. It's scary because it's not logical. And *logical* is how most psychiatrists, scientists, judges — most of us try to figure things out. We let what we call logic erase the things that connect us. Erase what I want to call the metaphor of reality. The reality of seeing our creative connection in a blade of grass or that lump of clay just under the blade of grass. Pola is just a lot of the time speaking that way. They — Johnny and Pola — were living that way."

"Living like that," Romi wants to say, "must be like *being in* the thing, and not out there like some objective philosopher *looking at* the thing. But in your institutions, your Carduelis, reason says that half the time she is trying to kill herself. What's the clue?"

"What's the clue? That's a funny thing to say. The clue, I guess, is knowing the difference between the two languages, when one is not even a language."

"Come on, that's like juggling eggs with rocks."

"Look," Janivik answers, "I know I am flailing with a bunch of hopeless conundrums, but I have to do it. Maybe just for myself. The language that runs the institutions and the computers of the world, moves from predicate to predicate to predicate. And to do this it puts names on everything: schizophrenia is a disease, a disease is schizophrenia. Here, take this one: Women die; you are a woman; you will die. Now take this one: Grass dies; Women die; Women are grass."

Romi follows Janivik with an osmosis of gentle laughter. "Logic says I'm dead. Metaphor says I am grass." Reflecting the irony of that thought Romi traces her fingers over the surface of a round stone that decorates the table where she stands. Suddenly smiling again she looks back up at Janivik. "I would love to be grass."

"Maybe that's the clue," Janivik smiles, but his eyes blink uncertainly across the far wall. "But it's not clue enough."

"Maybe the clue is, waiting for the grass to grow." Sooner than she said it, Romi wants to take her words back. They don't work.

"The little monster is 'treatment,'" Janivik says, "The predicate 'schizophrenia' is like the predicate *'will die'* attached to *Pola*. 'Classification.' We would have connected differently before 'classification.' Or before the linear-predicating model of the language we use and live by."

Romi bites her lip concealing her amusement. "That's a hard one. That's like getting outside of evolution, time, and the whole culture."

"No, no," Janivik laughs, "the wonder of language, culture— god, no! You and I are talking about the misappropriation of those models. Allowing those models to run in linear and dividing directions, splitting us from the sacred unity of mind and nature, asking us to navigate only in the isolate world of reason, forbidding our journey into the chaos of the deep unconscious; denying the healing placelessness of the mandala, the koan paradox, and, and— Pola's synchronicity with Valjonni, her metaphorical images — whatever you want to call them — my own forlorn dreamscape."

Romi is quietly stunned by Janivik's flow of words and his confession -she concludes- of being caught-up in Pola's dreamscape. She wants to chide him. "You're many words have only said precisely why it's hard."

" For me it is hard. For Pola it's different. Her trauma takes her there. It's like the natural thing in Nature. A splinter in her finger gets infected. The phagocytes, those big white blood cells come along and wall off the wound, ingest the microbes and the other foreign stuff and she gets stronger than she ever was. It's not biological or the same, but sometimes a similar correction system works to releave madness or what people like Doctor Gass call madness. We have the ability to put the trauma to sleep with drugs, and sometimes we don't have any choice, because we don't understand or can't honor something so foreign as caring. For someone, not so bloody-gone, and with simmering mandala questions like Pola, putting the questions to sleep with big drugs denatures her — even puts her sexuality to sleep — shelters her from those wonderfully creative constellations of connection, and puts her behind a dark wall of rationally built fences. Without a society that understands this we have no guides, no daring, none of that forgiving tolerance we sometimes call love." Janivik takes a long weary breath, conscious again that he is ranting. "Pola can't do it alone. None of us can. She is divided. We are divided. So we still insist that the brain, the mind, the body and that unadulterated field of grass are just so many unrelated entities. It's her Art, Pola's Art, that was destroyed in another life, that gives me the clue. She is my guide."

Romi shifts uneasily in her chair. She looks down at her knees and rubs the fingers of one hand against both eyebrows at once, then she checks his face again. "Are you telling me you are in love with her."

"I'm only saying that's how far it goes. I have to hear from her in that kind of empathy, and she has to hear from me the same." Janivik has a sudden flare of anger, "No Holy Matrimony of some puppy, daddyfied, bloody love. Dammit. Don't say things like that. She tells us things about ice angels, story-telling clay figures, intuitive-snakes and mystery-keepers. Its Homer's Odysseus returning to the cave of Nymphs. Something goddam timeless is going on here. I have even seen that 'cross,' the sex-finger-cross she painted one time. I've seen it on some paleolithic cave wall. Some of these things are like the guts we are born with."

Romi's eyes widen as she studies Janivik's driving immersion in Pola's journey. No not journey, she tells herself. This whole incredible immersion in a timeless mythology. "You know when you said, back there, the 'outside of time' thing? Something hit me. Pola wants to say so much that Valjonni did these things. Did he? How much of this is all Pola, and how much, if any, is Valjonni. I want to ask, what could such communication be. I want to ask does this immersion mean Pola and Valjonni can be in some kind of direct communication even now? Or that these mandalas and such are some kind of healing messages that he has left for her, somehow, or somewhere in the void, or what? Have you ever heard of re-emergent ESP? I'm not ready to say he is communicating from behind the vale, but, 'outside of time', in that dreaming place, so empty of logic, and she is listening, or she can 'tune-in' anytime she feels desperate?" Romi's whole tone is tentative, insecure, but she wants to make her case. "You know— if it's out there like that, then it should be there, even for us."

Janivik looks at Romi curiously. "You are not talking clairvoyant communication with a dead man? Or are you talking retro-cognitive clairvoyance. I've heard some of the ESP people talk about this."

Romi pinches her chin into a strange little dent. "I'm really talking 're-emergent' clairvoyance. Or, I guess it could be retro-cognitive, too. Something that is personally subliminal but part of the larger, what Jung was calling it; the Universal Unconscious. Outside of time —? Stays outside of time? Is still there.

"But I don't know how Pola's detail fits in here," Romi pauses. "Have you ever been out there? Are there any artifacts of these things she talks about? Does the world she is constructing really include his — his Mind things? If, as we seem to be saying, there's no duality. Then we might find something, you know, something that could be in harmony with what she's been telling us in her Mind things. Can't those Mind things, like Pola's art be out there? You know what I mean — *art-a-facts?* Why don't we try it!"

"Try what?"

"Find out if any of her stories really happened. Or maybe something about their missing parts."

"You mean like dancing a mandala in a tower? How impossible can you get?

"Umm — would be difficult."

"But it isn't a thing," Janivik insists on reminding her. "It's the *meaning*, and she has to find it."

"Just the same ... maybe there's a connection. Maybe not a mandala, but maybe something he made for her. It was around Christmas you know."

"Oh, god, Romi! It would be like looking for the Holy Grail. Whatever it is, *if* it is, is something personal, some image that Valjonni used in his own deliverance."

"But you think they shared a life in that cave, right?

"They shared a lot. Or maybe Pola is living in some very vivid dream. Whatever it is, it's her experience now. It's Pola who tells the stories. And she has to make her own discoveries."

Chapter Thirty-five

Four days after Romi had finished another meditation instruction with the prisoners who come to The Gateless Gate, she still felt disappointed that Janivik saw no need to go to the Ice Cave, to at least touch the ground where Pola had been. And she could not stop thinking of the Koan she had used with the prisoners from the Gateless ... Book of Zen Koans. The one that made her feel so helpless: About 'the man who hangs from a tree only by his mouth. If he answers the important question, he falls to his death.' But the "important question" she thinks is in another Koan: 'If a person argues and searches for something more than the fact, he is a man of dualistic concepts and will never grasp the fact.' That sums it up Romi tells herself. For Janivik, that might be 'dualism': to go to the cave and become a Sherlock. But the next day it all changed.

Pola had come to the barrier again, and because she was coming to it more often and with less emotion, Janivik had asked her if it would help her to see this *'something.'* if she went back to the Ice Cave.

"No! No! I can't do that! You've got to help me! You've — " her pleading eyes were all that Janivik could see. Then:

" She strangely paused," Janivik tells Romi, "and her whole emotion faded, like out of the blue, she said, 'Why didn't you go with Romi when she asked you to go out there?' Romi watches the wave of suspicion and bafflement cross his face when next Janivik speaks: "How did she know this? How did she know this?"

"This is eerie," Romi says. "Can we go?"

Chapter Thirty-six

Going to the Ice Cave was not just another exploration for Romi and Janivik. First they had visited with Kate and then with Norton, the stone mason, to find the way. Traveling on the back-country roads of the United States Forest Service, roads mainly kept open for fire protection, was a journey into a wildness and a vastness which totally distracted them from the little hand-drawn map Romi had sketched for their guide. And Romi's sense of place and how to get there was always different from Janivik's. Janivik's was, he thought, the rule of compass. Romi's way was more ingeniously inside a mirrored web. It was neural, it was tactile, something between the left and right brain he thought, an ephemeral tapestry that she could remember like her skin once she had been there, but something they usually could not communicate between them. That's why Romi usually drove. When your navigating, one language should be better than two. Romi was satisfied to call herself dyslexic, and, like now, when they were lost, she sighed and held her hand up to shape the letter "L," to follow the other "L" she'd written on the map. But being lost was what they longed for and didn't speak. Seductively, the dimming light led them into a path, a four-wheeler kind of road that appeared to go up and up over ragged gully-washed rocks of pegmatite and feldspar. It was unlikely their little Toyota could straddle all the crystalline horns of sharp stone that appeared like birthing mountaintops in the center of the road. At least in this light it would be a trick.

They stepped out of the car and drank from a carafe of dark coffee, contemplated the clear and soon to be starry night, glanced into the backseat of the car at the plaid comforter that was always there, had often sheltered them in urgencies of cunt and cock.

The night would play its darkness. The mystery would have another edge. They might have made a nest of sprigs and bows, but they did not.

The fallen needles from this crest of Limber Pine was quite enough, and little time there was to wait for touching.

The heat of waiting had begun somewhere on the road, had blinded them perhaps. And now the Forest is a sky-born tent where nakedness is sheltered. They have no picture, no memory, of how their jeans, their shirts, their panties disappeared. Their tongues were thrusting in each other's mouth, and then her tongue withdrew and hungered on a liquid path of searching to the root, his avid root. And when it did, they fell together. His lips, his teeth, his tongue mapping in tangled sweetness and ferocity the tendril flesh and amber memory. Explicit as an "O" ring, her lips junctured with his beam of beaming urgency, went firm against his phallic sac, his balls near bruised with aching pleasure. In centimeters her lips pulled a constant, slowly, sliding suck – Janivik helpless in her mouth – until she reached the flaming end, where then, her mouth still tight around his swollen cord, she rolled her tongue in firm appraisal. And with her naked hand, she grasped and pulled the mountain from her mouth in one exploding heaven. Then, sucked and licked and ate the cum that came in spurting spurts. Her eyes vague focused on a distant planet, she passed her wolfish tongue along her lips, where tears were also spread.

That night, they were soon to wake again. The moon still naked on their knees. Some dream Janivik must realign with this reality of Romi and himself. He touches her, and she is waiting. This time there will be no interlude. His cock intent as a plowman's share. And she is waiting, waiting. Dripping. Yet, something curious: Blond innocence has sweetened all the air. A woman is seated on the gray rock beside their blanket. A mentor. Blessing what they will do, have done. Strangely, as a mother, proudly — approving her daughter's technique, her daughter's consummate pleasure. But this is not a mother, nor is it innocence. The mystery mentor is very young and very blond.

Nothing matters. Only meaning. The voluptuary angel endorsing every move. It grows and grows. This thrust of one and two and three, through gateless gates of fervent membrane. It is a dream and not a dream, as Romi soon will tell.

○

The mountain chill sharpens with the rising sun and there is very little coffee left. Romi thinks she sees the roof of a fire tower somewhere near the top of this rocky trail and they agree to stir their ragged bodies with a hike to see the view.

The tower appears to be empty and they climb its zagging metal steps to the top. The view is grand, and then they look inside the windowed cabin where Janivik sees the circled glass of a triangulation disc, the spinning table that the lookout ranger would use to find the geography of a smoke flare. "Hey, maybe we could use that map — find out where we are," Romi says.

"That map, that spinning thing, is exactly what Pola described, flashing from the lightning in the middle of Valjonni's mandala dance. Wow," Janivik says, trying to compose himself. He begins searching around the catwalk, but finds all the doors and windows are locked. "Well, I guess we didn't leave anything in there anyway." When they survey the view again, they see some roads that might relate to Romi's penciled map. The jumping off place was to be a game trail near a creek on the north of a three way gravel junction. They could see a three-way junction, and now they knew which way was north.

○

The animal trail was an obvious, ancient path along the top of a radically eroding ridge of deep red clay. Other dendrites of passage led into it from deep within the forest. Below the ridge, a creek wound its way and joined another larger creek which they followed into a changing landscape of limestone knobs and castles. Coming over another hill they looked straight ahead into a groin of merging vales. And pointing down between the vales, Janivik asked Romi if she could see the dark horizontal chasm that opened there, "... like a giant horizontal cunt," he said. They walked silently to its edge, like two beans magnetized with magic, and stopped.

Inside, the light was beginning to catch the ice crusted-pool at the foot of the Ice Angel. And they could hear the tinkle of water dripping from the cavern's broad ceiling and from the Angel's icy arms as they walked down and into the darkening space. With each step, the hollow, metallic sounds of the limestone shards that covered the floor tumbled and echoed in a clean and solemn sanctuary voice. The Angel itself was still half-again taller than Janivik, but must have been much taller in the heart of winter, he thought. Already thinking of the giant stalagmite as an angel, Janivik studies Her "She could have lived here a thousand years: melting and freezing, freezing and melting," he says, as he looks at the Angel's prismatic head and her strangely lifting arms. "Their sanctuary," Janivik says in a voice that is both reverential and flat. But how it evolved fascinates him — " her playhouse, his refuge, and *their sanctuary*." Romi listens but grows silent, and then they are both silent. It's not just contemplation that holds them in this silence. Maybe a kind of hypnosis. The outer world draining away and the underworld taking over. A serpent language, from inside the earth itself.

They hadn't yet begun to search around, had not really noticed the fallen poles that might have been Valjonni's wikiup. Though there was some unacknowledged question in their heads about the stakes and rectangular divots that had the appearance of some student archaeological project, and the burned logs that might have been Valjonni's, or from the campfire of some passing hunter.

One of the misbegotten logs, a burl or maybe a root, lay just under the crust of ice at the edge of the melting Angel's pool. In her eyes, Romi sees art in the contours of its stony shape. She cannot lift her eyes from what she sees. Suddenly, she cannot resist exclaiming: "The Ice Man!" She lets her eyes be drawn into that shadowed image beneath the crust of ice. When she speaks the same words again, it rings like a question not daring to be an epiphany.

His eyes still hovering on the melting stalagmite, Janivik is slow to see Romi's apparition, but when he turns to really see, he is stricken. Stricken and without words.

They pull the figure from the ice, and turn it, and turn it. Seeing, but not knowing what to speak. What to say of its dormant somatosense, its hypsistarian complexity. In Zen, Romi guesses it would be a complex of things and no complex of things, as in — 'only emptiness has form, and only form is empty,' but she does not want to confront it as anything but found-art, a thing that perhaps meant something important to Valjonni, if, indeed, he is the one who brought it here.

Chapter Thirty-seven

The "Head," as he now called it is in no way a simple piece of found-art, in Janivik's perception. It has a haunting connection to his own dream-image of an archaic being who was never ever, quite visible in his own journeys of the night. He could not bring it to Pola, at least not yet. Not without more time for Janivik's own contemplation. And in that contemplation, he even wonders: This is not Janivik and Romi bringing the "Head" to Pola. It is Pola bringing the "Head" to Janivik and Romi. "This is a little crazy," Janivik again reminds himself, when he realizes that it is probable that Pola has never even seen it. But why does this simple piece of wood so fill both Romi and himself with such a cast of senseless awe?

○

At their home Janivik places the "Head" on the mantel, like the bust of some Laertes. Seeing it in every light or angle, in each new perspective, it makes its changes: Nobility and Death, a Serpent risen from the underworld, a Cronos melding earth and sky, and all-in-all a universal Psyche, the Soul that made it The Four-in-Three. He knew it was nuts to think or especially talk about a burl, a root of wood this way, except to Romi. With her it was easy. And, together, they found themselves calling it the Psyche Head. The pervading question still remained: "Is this the "Mystery Keeper" Valjonni, the mud sculptor, saw.

"In his trauma," Romi said, "I think a kind of sixth sense maybe went into gear, and this weirdly transforming image became his communicant, how he bonded with the Forest. And in it, with Pola, there was this need for Valjonni to share it with the 'other side.' Nothing works without the 'other,' right?"

Janivik laughs, "Pretty funny: Pola and polarity."

Romi smiles, "Well you know, things do come together that way." She looks again at the enigmatic bust on the mantel, then walks across the room, studying it as she goes. "It's not so hard to see it as a 'touchstone,' at least not for me. Or for someone like Valjonni, the mud sculptor, who must have lived in that open, searching place. Look: When I see this side, I see an absolute skull, a kind of ghoulish — risen from the grave — figure of death, for sure. And, as I cross over I see this transformation into nobility, the root of life, primitive, enduring, timeless. And yet it is of a *piece*, always this head we want to call the Psyche Head. But, then, look at its long curving neck, which makes the whole root look like a serpent, a creature from the underworld that has just now burst from a crack in the rocks. And, and touch it, it is like stone!"

Janivik silently marvels at Romi's engagement with this 'thing' as she strides across the room in front of it. Finally, she wants to sum it up. "*If you could touch the whole forest with one hand, it would be this root.*" But just as Romi sits down again, Pola quite surprisingly enters the door.

Pola has seldom been out of Carduelis by herself, and she has never come to visit Romi or Janivik on her own. Janivik, feeling oddly embarrassed that their indulgence has kept them from going directly to Pola with the 'root,' has a sudden remembrance of his Presbyterian mother's surprise visit when he and his debauching friends had littered every surface of their summer cabin, door steps to attic, with open bottles of booze and derelict paraphernalia. But with Pola, the surprise is easily allayed in a brevity of hugging and the silent irresistible turning of heads – a gathering together of their possible connection on the mantel. Could this have really been what Valjonni had hoped to bring Pola that fatal December?

So many names, but Pola immediately sees it as Valjonni's oracular hunter: The Mystery Keeper, the Four in Three.

She begins crying. Crying, and smiling. Crying and walking like a younger person. For several minutes she walks in sunwise circles before the enigmatic Head, seeing it, Janivik could imagine, for all the faces of the Forest it might project to her, or, her to it.

○

When, at last, Pola stops circling and finally looks at Romi and Janivik, they are still waiting for what she would say. Then, with uncharacteristic calm and confidence she speaks. "This was, this is —." Interrupting herself, she looks again for a long time at the 'root,' then continues, "This is, I know this is what Johnny brought." She looks around the room in a strangely reflective way, and then thoughtfully at Romi and Janivik. With a decisive nod of her head she announces her intent: "And, now, we must take Her back. The Forest would want this Old Woman back."

Chapter Thirty-eight

"There is nothing that the madness of men invents that is not either nature made manifest or nature restored.
Michel Foucault, from *Madness and Civilization*

Janivik arranged that Pola could stay with Romi and Janivik that night, where she would sleep on the couch in that same room with Johnny's root. Carduelis expected her back and she would return. But in the morning, the three of them, with the Mystery Keeper, returned to where the Head had been found. Carrying it wrapped in a blanket, Pola would not touch it.

○

At the Ice Cave she calmly studied how Johnny might have placed it there before the smoke-bombs forced him out. She had heard the witnesses tell how he had crossed the creek twice. And, now, she was able to recall the detail of how she saw Johnny fall from the bullet that entered his back. That place, at the edge of the creek, where he fell, was where she would return Johnny's Mystery Keeper. At that place she put it down on the tall dry grass. Unfurled it from the blanket. Lifted it. And carried it to the creek, where, like a child sending its sailboat onto the water, she watched it float away. Away, she hoped to where he had first seen it as he drank with the snake from this creek.

The Annotated Pola

I had not intended this publishing of an "Annotated Pola." It had originally been sketched as an aid to editing the 'Pola' manuscript. But when both the editor and the publisher subtly suggested making these notes part of the whole, I concluded that my writing was so damnably obscure it needed this other dimension. But flattering myself I realized that a whole genre of storytelling erupted when *The Annotated Alice* was created, and we learned that the author of *Alice in Wonderland* didn't know where Alice was going when she went down the rabbit hole, and that Lewis Carroll, that author, carried clothespins to the beach just in case some little girl might need her skirt pinned up to save it from getting in the surf. Then realizing that I was a far more conventional author than the man who let Tweedledum and Tweedledee recite a poem when all Alice wanted were directions out of the rabbit hole, I simply let my armor down by agreeing to put it up again.

Lewis Carroll (Author, Christ Church College, Oxford), John Tenniel (Illustrator), Martin Gardner (Editor, Annotator of the Notes).

Chapters 1-3

All of this is obviously 'establishing' character and location while presenting the question of Pola. But it is also establishing a coordinate for exploring the ecology of art mind and nature by initiating its form in the metaphorical language of mythology, a language which will appear to some as cinematic. Indeed, the ethnologist Claude-Levi Strauss noted that the telling of many of human-kind's earliest myths were or are in the present-tense, as though they were happening now, 'like cinema,' he said.

Add to this that some of humankind's creation myths use the images of feces as the material of primal creation, the very material of our planetary existence. In a way that might be described as both creative and regressive, Pola is painting a mandala from feces. And mandalas in many forms, including the narrative, become Pola's journey.

Also, these first chapters introduce the dichotomy of the 'double-bind,' which might be called the antagonist in this story.

Although we are witnessing Pola's 're-emergent' expressions, her very direct revelations from her life with Johnny Valjonni, how that process works is speculative. Within this whole idea of *art, mind and nature — a sacred unity* comes the necessary realization of a whole-swimming communion or communication, and that realization finds a powerful presence as we are allowed to see into Pola's visionary journey. In this, Pola appears to become one with Johnny Valjonni as in the mandala dance that happens in a storm -stricken fire-lookout tower.

Chapter 4

Dr. Janivik's earlier experience with another woman who had reached from madness into sanity without drugs now believes he has found her parallel in Pola; and almost like an evangelist he is struggling against the conventional pharmaceutical approach at this 'behaviorist' oriented mental health center, Carduelis.

Chapter 11

Like a contagion, the psychiatrist, Janivik, has been drawn into the hallucinatory life of Pola. The dream he is waking from has been triggered by the ongoing involvement he is having with Pola, and it is being explored by his own intellectual speculation into the dynamics of other mythological voyagers. At first, he was not so overtly doing this. But Pola has made Janivik her Valjonni, and her extraordinary imagery has driven Janivik into the labyrinth of her journey. Although Pola's journey has entered into Janivik's unconscious, it is there, too, because Janivik consciously understands the necessity for Pola to have a guide in this nether-land if she is to somehow breakthrough her madness. They are by now on this journey together. Later, or gradually, Romi, Janivik's partner, gets drawn in with her own Zen orientation, and the mystery sets Romi, Janivik and the reader adrift in the melange of identity, meaning and interpretation. From this point the narrative becomes a sort of detective story of going to the center of the center to the center – where some keeper of mystery now resides for each of them in a communal psyche.

Chapter 13

Here it is mostly the subjective privacy of Pola's depression we are sharing. She is alone, and we see only what she sees. No real dialog, just the darkness that still seems to be coming from the life in the Forest where she and Valjonni lived. *Articulate speechlessness* Janivik calls it. Is it Valjonni's view, or Pola's view; is it a soldier's traumatic construction, or a non-combatant's, it doesn't matter. It is her experiential language of Valjonni's hopelessness war that draws Pola into 'emptiness.'

Chapter 14

In this chapter we are apprised of the "behaviorist" philosophy of the administrator, Dr. Gass, at this place where Janivik has come to work. It is also clear that Janivik is here almost by coincidence, having come to a nearby Zen Center and fallen in love with a teacher there.

Chapter 15

Janivik's struggle with Gass to keep Pola off drugs reaches another climax when she continues with her suicidal episodes.

Chapter 16

Here we are revealing more of Janivik's reflections and questions while expanding on the history of what we should know about Pola and Valjonni. After playing kung fu games with Romi and Janivik Pola tells very rational stories of how she met Valjonni and of his episode of going to his fugitive life in the forest. At the end of the chapter, Janivik thinks she is falling to sleep and leaves. But as the story moves into the next chapter (17) we find her not sleeping but entranced with her memories of meeting Valjonni, reenacting them in a private, reflective, but not really hallucinatory way.

Chapter 17

Pola slips back to the present moment , almost expecting to see her memory-train continue, but she sees only the walls of that padded cell.

Chapters 18, 19 and 20, 21, 22

The manuscript takes license to see the other, perhaps Roshomon-like, perspectives from the community where Pola and Valjonni lived and experienced much of the violence that has formed them, and has continued to haunt them. I want to show that community for its own paranoid and fantastical darkness, and its many perceptions of Valjonni. They hardly knew about Pola, but Pola secretly knew two sides of the story — the community and Valjonni. We have to get inside the things that brought Valjonni down, and that means giving his life in the community its substance before he enters the Forest and slips into the rather mystical journey with mud sculpture and Nature and Pola. Fiction lets us do this   to see back around the corner. But, in a fairly gradual way, we see what Pola did not see. The story has other Tellers.

Chapter 23

This is the important expression of Pola's becoming alive and integrated in her's and Valjonni's connection. It is her turn to be the mud-sculptor. Memory and personal evolution could be enough, but there often seem to be shared things happening within the 'unconscious,' enough to say something 'retro-cognitive' or of a shared sense of the archetypal is going on. (Throughout there has been suggestion of some sort of extra-sensory communication, or that something about the Forest, Pola and Valjonni is so tightly related — the necessary unity which this story attempts to approach — that everything and everybody is inside each others boots.) We have in this chapter, that reference to the Loa Tze myth, which gives this unitary idea the dignity of Time.

Chapter 24

Janivik and Romi witness the formal mandalas of the Tibetan Monks, comparing them with Pola's naive projections.

Chapter 25

It takes imaging schizophrenia and the divided self to explain the crack between logic and metaphor, and how — *illogically* — metaphor might heal.

Chapter 26

Still amazed at Pola's brave explorations and the revelations that come like messages from her life in the Forest, Janivik sees both meaning and hopelessness in Pola's fantasy world.

Chapter 27

In my conception of the whole story I wanted to gradually weave time and space together so that we see Valjonni, not always through Pola or the community, but now Valjonni himself. Later, the story brings Janivik into it as more than a counselor, when, almost as a kind of 'contagion' he begins having his own dreams as an extension of Pola's quest. It seems to me that my own quest for Unity requires this bit of logical disdain.

Chapters 28, 29:

We know very well that Pola has shared and continues to immerse with Valjonni, but I want us to see Valjonni's own special response to his life in the Forest. I think he loses some reality if we only know him in Pola's perceptions. So here we begin with Pola's recollections and slide into the drama of events which let us know some of Valjonni's pain and craziness. He had to have been on the edge just as Pola is. This is a story about *crazy*. *Logic and furniture will not tell this story. The narrative itself is maybe cubist. Which sounds like a good idea to me, but I didn't plan it that way.*

Chapters 30, 31:
We are of course into Pola's empathy with Valjonni, which is all about the depression and downsliding that followed the destruction of his mud-sculpture quest. Critical to the whole story is the reference that Valjonni wants to 'choose his Hunter.' I feel it is a wonderfully inverse idea: Though he is hunting for some profound image he believes he has seen out there in the Forest, he views it equally as something that hunts him, something he will know when it happens. It seems to me it is a connection that goes beyond fate: He chooses it. It chooses him. Existential Unity?

Chapter 32
Christmas time, always a traumatic memory for Pola, finds a touching moment of communication, when Janivik taps out a rhythmic tone-poem of three notes on his own Christmas toy, a multiphonic, slit-drum. The three notes are open-ended like a question. And when he repeats the three notes, Pola grabs the drum mallet and completes the poem with a resounding *fourth* note. A climactic moment of 'the divided-self' finding connection, a moment that was joyful and evolving, but also orgasmic to the point of frightening Dr. Janivik.

The previous chapter sets up Valjonni's departure (about Valjonni going back to Cambria, at Christmas). Pola calls it 'creepy' and doesn't seem to really understand it. So it's back to Valjonni's perception and to detailing the events of his darkest and most profound encounters, and, eventually, his assassination.

Chapter 33
This becomes a kind of epistemological travel zone where the two wanderers with Pola are unraveling the puzzle of her seeming clairvoyance and the immersing qualities of metaphor as an explanation of her (our) world. This is where the narrative, which has used schizophrenia to show the 'split' now examines wholeness, unity, healing. The 'divided road' is

coming together. From the alienation we perhaps see something of the journey back to what, on the intellectual side of this, I have been calling *Art, Mind and Nature — a sacred Unity.*

Chapter 34

There is a struggle between pragmatism and intuition. Could there be more than fantasy in Pola's story-world. Pola in her desperation has reached into something equivalent to clairvoyance it would seem (the Natural world meeting the Natural world).

Chapter 35:

This blond woman in the sex dream, I believe, is both a 'releasing' and an 'endorsing' representative of Pola. The interwoven relationship with Pola and Janivik's shared journey has reached a creative conclusion. In this way Pola has set Janivik and Romi free to consummate her journey. (Was Janivik a little too much Valjonni?) The three, or the four, of them had issues that had to be leveled. Something very new and strange is about to happen.

Chapters 36 and 37:

The "Head," "The Four in Three," "The Mystery Keeper" is found. And there is an actual "Head," one that is visually convincing to this description and this story. It might better remain in its mythological realm. But it was truly found in the forest where this story has traveled, and it has been photographed in the context of this story.

fini of *Annotated Pola*

About the Author

Charles Nauman and his wife, Grete Bodøgaard, a tapestry artist, share a live-in studio in South Dakota. His writing has been published in the *Iowa Review* and *The Lakota Nation Journal.* His first book length work, *Hay Camp,* published by Dakota West Books, explored historical perspectives of the Black Hills. His poetry is widely anthologized.

As a film writer and director, Nauman's films have ranged from the feature, *Johnny Vik* (honored at Cannes, Locarno and the Prix L'Age D'Or in Brussels) to the experimental *Sitting Bull's Bones* with Stan Brakhage. His *Tahtonka* was an American Film Festival Blue Ribbon winner and the "Critic's Choice" for a BBC-TV reprise. In 2006 his film *Tarahumara: Festival of the Easter Moon,* was selected for several international festivals including Bilan du film ethnographique, Musee de l'Homme, Paris.

www.ingramcontent.com/pod-product-compliance
Lightning Source LLC
Chambersburg PA
CBHW071020180726
48291CB00004B/1557